Jessie felt an aura of danger in the air...

Throughout the brief conversation, she had been standing tensely, a tingle of alarm running through her senses. She watched cautiously, her ears straining for any foreign sound. Now her trained ears caught the faint click of a revolver coming to full cock.

Instantly she dived sideward, a shout of warning on her lips. A revolver blasted and its muzzle flame made a bright streak at the open doorway. Jessie rolled across the carpet, tugging open her tiny purse and grasping for her derringer. Some of the women were screaming, the men were shouting, and Senator Brockett was calling for her to take care.

Instead Jessie took aim...

◆— **WESLEY ELLIS** —◆

LONE STAR

AND THE BIGGEST GUN IN THE WEST

J (R)

A JOVE BOOK

LONE STAR AND THE BIGGEST GUN IN THE WEST

A Jove Book/published by arrangement with
the author

PRINTING HISTORY
Jove edition/August 1985

ISBN: 0-515-08332-1

Jove books are published by The Berkley Publishing Group,
200 Madison Avenue, New York, N.Y. 10016. The words
"A JOVE BOOK" and the "J" with sunburst are trademarks
belonging to Jove Publications, Inc.

PRINTED IN THE UNITED STATES OF AMERICA

Chapter 1

The great brass whistle screamed in a flurry of steam. Work-men began to pivot gangplanks aboard, and the paddle wheel mounted astern of the *Paiute* started to turn slowly, idly, prepatory for the command to depart. From the bridge the blue-coated captain was yelling himself hoarse with orders, while dockside, stevedores were coiling ropes. The *Paiute* rode heavy with cargo and a handful of passengers. It was a thousand-ton shallow-draft vessel painted red and white, the Starbuck colors, and its buffered snub-nosed prow pressed hard against the tail of three laden barges which soon it would be pushing down the Sacramento River.

Leaning against the deck rail was Ki, a lithe man in his early thirties whose features bore the handsome quality that appeals to women who like their men tempered by expe-rience and bronzed by sun. As usual Ki was dressed in normal range garb—faded jeans, loose-fitting collarless shirt, worn black vest, and battered Stetson. His feet were clad in Asian-style rope-soled cloth slippers, but in this land of sandals and moccasins, these were not remarkable. Nor were his almond-shaped eyes, straight blue-black hair, and that golden coloring which strongly suggested that his mother had been Japanese and his father a white American. In this Californian melting pot of blood and race, crossbreeding was too common to draw attention.

So, compared to the colorful melange of people around him, all quite busy, it wasn't surprising that those about Ki took little notice of him and showed even less interest. All except one: a tall, lissome woman in her twenties who stood on the dock waving a friendly farewell to him.

Unlike Ki, Jessica Starbuck was attired in finery, and her green tweed jacket and skirt did little to conceal her firm, jutting breasts and sensuously rounded thighs and buttocks. Her mother, Sarah, had been a redheaded beauty who'd passed to her daughter a long-limbed, lushly molded figure, flawless ivory skin, and a cameo face with a pert nose and a spark of feline audacity to her wide-set green eyes. And Jessie's father, Alex Starbuck, had given a steadfastness to her dimpled chin and a shrewd if sometimes humorous twist to her lips. Even though both parents were dead—murdered and subsequently avenged—in a quite real sense they lived on, embodied in the spirit and actions of their offspring.

Ki and Jessie had known each other since childhood when Alex Starbuck had hired Ki to be Jessie's companion and guardian. It had been a wise choice, for Ki, as an orphaned half-breed outcast in Japan, had been apprenticed to one of the last great samurai, Hirata, and had grown skilled in unarmed combat and in the use of bow and arrow, sword, staff, stick, and throwing weapons. Indeed, even now in his vest and pockets were stashed short daggers and other small throwing weapons, including a supply of *shuriken*, little razor-sharp steel disks shaped like six-pointed stars. Devoted to Jessie, and loyal to her far-flung inherited interests, Ki was to a great degree the protector behind the Starbuck throne. As such, he preferred being out of the limelight like this, passing unnoticed and attracting little if any attention.

For the next couple of days, however, Ki would not be beside Jessica, and he'd be more visible than he normally cared to be.

Trouble was plaguing the Indianhead Marine Transportation Company, owner and operator of the *Paiute* and four similar barge freighters—trouble in the guise of sabotage and river piracy, especially along the navigable stretch of the San Joaquin River that ran south of Sacramento down as far as Estero, the small port town deep in the heartland of the San Joaquin Valley. The rash of attacks had spiraled to the point where business suffered, the Valley farmers threatening to use other means to freight in supplies and ship out their wheat and produce. This had brought Jessie and Ki to Sacramento, for Indianhead was ultimately owned, through a series of holding companies and subsidiaries, by Starbuck. And the entire worldwide business conglomerate known as Starbuck was solely owned, in turn, by Jessica. The buck stopped with Jessie, and she was determined to put a stop to the trouble.

They'd traveled all the way from Jessie's Circle Star Ranch in Texas without incident, but once in Sacramento, Jessie had found it difficult to wriggle free of certain social obligations. They'd had to ask questions of various authorities, and with the answers—none of them, alas, of any use—had come invitations by important persons and state government officials to attend this function and that party. Jessie, being *the* Starbuck, simply couldn't decline them all; it would've been tantamount to a snub, and besides, things could be learned at such occasions.

Tonight, for example, Jessie would be attending one of those big, "intimate" dinners where everyone wore boiled collars or hoop-skirted crinolines. She was going as guest of honor of the hostess, Mrs. Willabelle, an elderly widow who was the grande dame of Sacramento's social circuit. Ki supposed he could have wangled an invitation, too, but getting duded up for very rich food and droning conversation was not his notion of a pleasant evening. Anyway, it made sense to ride one of the barge freighters, to get the feel of it and the course it took, and since the *Paiute* was scheduled to leave for Estero today, well . . .

3

So a plan was hatched whereby Ki would take the freighter to Estero and see what he could find out along the way. If possible, he'd then meet some of the Valley farmers, notably Gunther Mellon, who, by the number of complaining letters he'd sent, was evidently their local spokesman. In fact, in the last purple-prosed message Gunther had sent to Indianhead—and thence to Starbuck—he'd offered his ranch as a place to stay, in case any lazy, fat-arsed corporate bigwig cared a diddlysquat damn enough to show up and get the facts straight from the horse's mouth.

Jessie wasn't too sure from which end of the horse these facts might be coming, but she had replied that someone, most likely she and Ki, would soon visit. Under the circumstances Ki would now be acting like an advance man. Her part of the plan was to leave Sacramento on horseback either tomorrow or the day after, depending on whether she could get out of attending Senator Brockett's gala reception tomorrow afternoon.

That was the plan. Of course, Ki was well aware that life was what happened when one was making other plans. So was death...

Ponderously the sternwheeler nudged away from the pilings into the mainstream of the Sacramento River, shoving the clumsy barges before it. On the dockside quay, parasols went up and twirled above plumed hats, while small talk resumed and onlookers, including Jessie, sauntered toward their carriages and surreys.

Ki remained against the rail, feeling the throb of engines and the spray drifting from the paddle wheel. Gradually the boardwalks, gas lanterns, and brick-and-plank false-fronted buildings of downtown Sacramento slid past and then the lower, closer sprawl of ramshackle housing fell astern.

The town had certainly matured, he thought fleetingly. After its rambunctious start as a Gold Rush tent settlement beset by fire, flood, and cholera, the feverish search for quick riches had given way to steady though unspectacular development, Sacramento becoming first the terminus of the Pony Express, then the transcontinental railroad, as well as the capital of one of the most fascinating states in the union.

Mainly, though, Ki kept his eyes and thoughts centered on those who had boarded the *Paiute* with him. He'd made a point of being one of the very first aboard and had been standing at this railing while the others had climbed on, watching them, trying to size them as they swarmed to their respective places.

The majority, of course, were Indianhead employees— hands, a few officers, and one steward for the small number of passengers that the *Paiute*, like most freighters, carried along for extra revenue. None of the passengers was the Fancy Dan sort or the kind of ferret-eyed professional drifter type who plied the large riverboats. Mostly they were ranch and field laborers, boomers who'd turned to farm work after the gold fields had petered out. Some were thick-necked, thick-headed toughs who resembled Barbary Coast thugs from San Francisco and who could have a dozen different reasons—none of them savory—for being aboard. There was also a handful of haughty young men who looked as if they'd never done a lick of work and sashaying young ladies who looked as if their work were done mainly on their backs. Ki had an ingrown mistrust of them, male or female, not respecting anybody who felt softish.

Yet contempt was one thing, neglect another. Even the limpest of wrists can squeeze a trigger, and he was not about to be caught off guard by them if he could help it. Almost instinctively, as he viewed a swishy gentleman prance along the deck, he pressed his arm against where his *tanto*, his short, curve-bladed knife, was sheathed inside the waistband of his pants.

The freighter passed only one riverboat that morning,

the big sidewheeler *Delta Queen* that required plenty of clearance. Compared with it, the *Paiute* with its barges was sluggish. Yet the sternwheeler moved steadily with the current, and Ki didn't believe anything could stop them. Gunfire from shore would have little effect; the crewmen could take cover among the stacks of supplies. An attack with small boats like yawls or skiffs could be met and smashed with rifles. Even Ki's elementary knowledge of the river system hereabouts was enough to convince him that the danger point was the delta area just ahead.

Captain Irving was of the same opinion. He joined Ki on deck, as his first mate in the pilothouse above steered the *Paiute* into the series of waterways that cut a crisscross pattern among the overhanging sycamores, willows, and cottonwoods of the lush delta. It was here, in this so-called "Everglades of the West," that an attack by a band of determined raiders might meet with success—and where, not long before, just such an attack had occurred.

Ki remarked, "I don't see anything so far."

"If there's any rumpus a-brewin'," Captain Irving replied, "you won't until it happens. If it does, we'll be ready, I vouch."

To add emphasis, the captain canted his denim river cap over one eye, the cap having shrunken in size until it could no longer capture all the white hair of his shaggy head. His nose was cured a deep mahogany by river suns and winds, and the seams about his weathered face showed his years of battling nature as well as man.

With experienced foresight Captain Irving had armed his crew with carbines, bought at Starbuck expense, and had authorized any who wished to carry sidearms to do so. This applied not only to the hands aboard the *Paiute,* but also to those on the barges. There were four hands to each barge, whose customary duty was to use long poles to help keep the barges in line and to ward the crafts away from sandbars

6

and bottom-ripping crags. Moreover, each barge carried a store of food, so that the hands could eat on the way and do away with any stopovers. The hands ate in pairs, so that the others were always on guard—either with poles or with Winchesters.

Captain Irving commented, "You're from Texas, I understand, so perhaps you never heard of the River Rats. They was a gang of pirates that made life miserable along the Sacramento."

"Yes, I have heard of them, Captain. But it must be ten years since they were broken up. Why?"

"Well, if I didn't know better, I'd swear they was back in action again. It's been like 'em, leastwise, what with the burnin' of cargo and warehouses, the maraudin' of our ships, and the gen'ral terrorizin' of the Valley. Why, word has it that even the farmers and ranchers are being hit, hit hard, losin' stocks and crops."

"That's kind of odd, don't you think?"

"Yeah, it is rare for pirates to strike landowners also, and same holds true in reverse. Common owlhoots most always shy away from water sports. On tuther hand, it makes a peck o' sense if they're tryin' to put us outta business and are striking at them who deal with us, as well as us ourselves. Some of the farmers, though, they're reckoning it's vice versa, and the pirates are tryin' to bust them by stopping us from transportin' their freight. Either way or neither, them bastards are doing a good job of it."

"We'll get them, Captain, don't worry."

"I hope. We've haven't had much luck so far, and we've been doing as much as we can, Ki, as much as we can. Indianhead has set up patrols to watch where the gang has a penchant to strike. We've hired extra hands and armed them and installed some 'specially large lamps on the top deck for better night viewing. But it's damn nigh impossible to watch it all, though, and still carry on our reg'lar work."

7

Ki rubbed his chin thoughtfully. "Has anybody recognized any of the pirates?"

"No, they usually wear masks. The pirates, that is, not our crews or the passengers. For the most part, they leave the passengers alone, which is stranger still. Don't seem ever to steal anything, not that there's much to steal. They just destroy. Scandalous, sir, scandalous."

They were now beginning to leave the delta. Ahead was open river, the San Joaquin, with wooded patches and stretches of farmland. It was here at the delta where the San Joaquin, one of the Sacramento's confluents, joined the larger river on its rush westward into Suisun Bay and, eventually, to the Pacific through San Francisco Bay. No longer could the barges float alone with the current, but needed the power of the sternwheeler to push against the flow. It was also here, now, that the shrewd engineering built into the *Paiute* proved its worth. For regular freighters, the San Joaquin was only navigable year-round for fifty miles to Stockton, even though the river itself was some 350 miles long. To reach farther south upstream, the *Paiute* and its sister ships were built with flat bottoms and cropped sternwheels, so they were able to navigate in as little as two and a half feet of water. Indianhead boasted that its vessels drew so little water that they could float on a heavy dew, although with the increasing use of the river for irrigation, this claim was being put to a sore test.

There seemed no danger ahead, but uneasiness seemed to grip Captain Irving. He shouted to the pilothouse, "Sharp eye, y'hear, sharp eye!" Then, as if that were not sufficient, he bade Ki to excuse him and began clambering up to the pilothouse, grumbling fretfully to himself, "Never can tell when or how they'll hit. Always a new wrinkle, them devils..."

The sun was a red ingot in the mid-afternoon sky. There was plenty of light for shooting, but the *Paiute* swept on and no attack came. Ki breathed more easily. The danger point, the delta, had been traversed, and Stockton was not far ahead.

The sun continued its slow arc toward the western horizon and was at a late-afternoon angle when the *Paiute* arrived at Stockton. The first two barges were left here at the local Indianhead depot, where their shipments of supplies would be off-loaded and, in due time, sacks of wheat would be on-loaded for a return trip. It was almost thrashing season in the Valley, and soon farmhands would be busy in the surrounding golden fields, while square-rigged English grain ships would lie at anchor in Sacramento to take on this profitable cargo.

The *Paiute* and its one remaining barge pushed on. The sun descended into evening, long-slanting shadows began turning opaque on the river, and the flat hills gradually lost their color.

"It's getting late," Ki said to Captain Irving when the captain happened by. "Are you about ready to tie in for the night?"

"Another three hours," Irving replied, "and we'll be at Estero, and'll have this trip finished. That's where we'll tie."

Night came. The steady beating of the boat's paddlewheel on the dark water took them through a rippling wheat ocean with patches of woods and rocks and occasional lantern-lit windows. The moon was three-quarters full and cast a silvery light, so it was easy to see the course ahead as the San Joaquin wound roughly southward. Now and then along the banks appeared barbed wire fences, their faintly shining strands strung on tree-trunk posts. A breeze rustled the high wheat which stretched eastward and westward into the black distance.

The darkness hid the crews from each other, but, in a cheery mood, they kept in touch by shouting back and forth.

Their weapons were at hand, yet they were relaxed, the trip about over, and no more threat of attack forseen.

Suddenly a curdling roar resounded along the river. Ki felt it as well as heard it and saw the flash of igniting powder. The grain and weedy grasses growing thick along both banks began to smolder, sending up dense waves of gagging smoke that swiftly enveloped the *Paiute*. Like a ghostly armada, the stenchy clouds of burning grasses were hauled out into the current of the river, directly into and against the path of the oncoming barge and freighter.

A great moaning whistle erupted from the *Paiute*. Captain Irving came running from the bow, his face contorted with rage. "The lousy, ship-scampin' sons!" he bellowed at Ki, as he started clambering up to the pilothouse. "It's an ol' Mississippi trick they're pullin', usin' black powder and rafts loaded with wet grass to blind us and make us heel aground!"

The freighter shuddered as its engines braked, but there wasn't enough time to stop and then reverse. The stern-wheeler and its barge slid into the massive, drifting cloud of smoke, driving full ahead toward God only knew what, for nobody could see.

The freighter's keel scrunched against the rocky bed of the low river, no longer able to navigate the thin, curving channel between the multitude of snags and sandbars. Her bow lifted and held high for a moment and fell, the barge slamming backwards, its impact helping to shock some of the forward momentum. Again the *Paiute* scraped bottom, this time crunching to a complete halt, throwing Ki off-balance. Around him was pandemonium—the hysterical cry of the few women, the shouting of men, and the penetrating blast of steam escaping from safety valves.

Then silence swiftly came—the first reaction from the freighter stopping dead in the water. The next instant, ropes with hooks snagged the rails, and kerchief-masked men

10

swarmed aboard from skiffs—just like the River Rats Captain Irving had mentioned.

The pirates were armed to the teeth, and most were carrying burning pitch torches. They heaved them at anything that might burn, the torches showering among the cargo and down the gangways. And as soon as they'd tossed their fiery brands, they opened up with their weapons, not aiming to slaughter but to terrify, although not caring if they killed in the process.

In quick response the rattled crews regrouped and started firing back. The pirates turned their bullets on them, pinning the crewmen down so they couldn't grab the torches and toss them overboard. All the while they smashed glass and furnishings and whatever else they could, as if trying to destroy the barge and freighter before the fires consumed them.

From high up came salvos of carbine fire, as Captain Irving and those with him in the pilothouse tried to pick off pirates and not the frantic passengers. Ki also joined in the battle, his eyes focused acutely with the charge of danger and blood. When he saw the figures leaping aboard, he began flinging *shuriken* at them the way a gambler would deal a deck of cards, with short, sharp flicks of his wrist that sent the steel disks spinning with deadly accuracy.

The nearest pirate to Ki, squeezing the trigger of his revolver, felt the twin jarring impacts of its recoil and the tearing of his flesh. He yelled wildly, as if disbelieving he could have been slashed by a whirling razor, falling backwards into the arms of another raider, who pushed him aside and leveled his own pistol at Ki. And Ki, seeing the gaping maw of this second revolver swing toward him, whipped his free hand toward his lethal throwing daggers. He threw one. He threw quickly and accurately, his knife and the raider's bullet virtually crossing in midair. But Ki had the satisfaction of seeing his blade hit—of seeing hands go up

11

in front of the man's face, the pistol dropping from nerveless fingers, the spouting blood welling from between them as the man collapsed atop his *shuriken*-slain comrade.

Meanwhile flame licked higher and spread swiftly across the decks of the freighter and barge. The night's breeze caught the fire and carried it out and on; the redness spread hungrily over the crafts, now fanning up dry timbers to the pilothouse.

Their task accomplished, the raiders sent a murderous barrage of their weapons as a covering fire for their escape. Dragging their wounded and dead with them, they vanished overboard and to the riverbanks under the cloak of their smoking rafts.

For a moment Ki stood listening to the cries of the frenzied passengers and the lurid cursing of the crew and Captain Irving. It was obvious the *Paiute* was doomed, and there was nowhere to go but into the river. Panic-stricken passengers and crew retreated over the side, floundering in the water shoreward and gathering in groups along the bank, quiet now and oddly drained of their emotion. A sullen roaring came out of the freighter. The night turned crimson, and this crimson fell across the pall of smoke rising from the still burning grass and the freighter's tortured hull.

Behind them, away from the river and low against the blackness of naked hills, were the scattered lights of Estero. At Ki's side, Captain Irving gestured toward the distant town and growled, "We might as well pack up and head there. It's a lost cause here."

Ki moved his shoulders. The captain was right; there was nothing he or anyone else could do.

After a short rest period, Captain Irving led the others from his still burning ship, forging a trail across the seemingly endless wheat fields. He held a steady pace, ignoring the complaints from a few of the softer passengers and exchanging an occasional word with his crew or with Ki.

Back at the river the crimson climbed higher and spread wider through the night, and heat came from the *Paiute* in a long swelling wave which drove them farther away.

Terror and death had struck the San Joaquin Valley. Not for the first time, and not for the last...

Chapter 2

While Ki was trudging doggedly toward Estero, Jessica was being transported in style to dinner.

The Acme Royal cabriolet carriage, which had been sent to pick up Jessie at her hotel, rolled through the American River Drive area with its distinguished estates and picturesque views of the river. Soon it turned into a wide lane and stopped before a pair of elaborate iron gates. The driver called to the gatekeeper, who swung open the gates at once and gave them a smiling salute as they drove into the grounds owned by Mrs. Willabelle.

Her mansion was built around three sides of a court, set in extensive lawns and gardens, and surrounded by large eucalyptus trees. A white-wigged footman met them at the front door and escorted Jessica into a pleasant room, furnished in the Louis XIV manner. As they entered, the footman announced her, and an elderly lady crossed to greet her.

The woman was rotund with plump thighs and gelatinous breasts, which even her tightly-strung whalebone corset couldn't keep still. From embroidered neckband to leather boot-toe, she was a butterball of black satin and silk—as befitting a wealthy widow—yet her round, cherubic face, framed by white hair, was anything but somber.

"Miss Starbuck," she said, smiling cordially, "I am delighted to have you here this evening. It's such an honor."

"The honor is mine, Mrs. Willabelle, and so is the delight."

There were six others in the room, and in due course another four people arrived and were announced. Mrs. Willabelle introduced Jessie to them all, a polite but mostly unnecessary ritual, for Jessie had already met many of them before. She was rather well acquainted with one man in particular, Senator Charles Brockett, who looked elegant as well as distinguished in gray fancy worsted and ruffled silk. He was average in features and build, but too much of a politician not to be vain; and although Jessie knew him to swagger when drunk, sober he was charming and smiled often.

Senator Brockett was smiling now, mainly at Jessie. Whereas the other women were generally clad in high-bodiced, ankle-length dresses, Jessie was garbed in the empire style that was the absolutely latest fashion at the time, and her gown, which left her arms and the upper part of her bosom exposed, set off her admirable figure. Her lustrous coppery-blonde hair was drawn through a gold ring at the back of her head and fell in curls on her neck. Her green-flecked eyes were ringed by dark lashes, which with her smooth eyebrows emphasized the delicate transparency of her skin. Something about its flawless texture seemed to fascinate the senator.

Noticing, albeit ignoring, his ill-concealed interest, Jessie bemusedly wondered what Brockett would think of her if he learned she was packing a pistol. A very small pistol, a two-shot .38 derringer to be exact, tucked discreetly in her chatelaine purse.

Dinner proved to be a gala affair. The dining room's huge gas chandelier had been cleaned and polished until it dazzled the eyes. The carved paneling and the scrolled velvet-covered chairs set off to perfection the handsome mahogany table. The service, too, was perfect. The menu began with

15

turtle soup and turbot and continued on through rumps, ham, tongue, venison haunches and fowl, all washed down with vintage Bordeaux and other fine wines.

The twelve elite diners sat at the long table, eating and drinking and exchanging polite gossip about mines, agriculture, and politics—the stuff upon which Sacramento thrived. Yet it seemed to Jessie that there was a strained air, a vague undercurrent of tension, about the occasion. She kept up her part of the conversation but sat there alertly, every nerve attuned.

At the conclusion of the feast Mrs. Willabelle ushered her guests into her drawing room, which looked across a gently sloping lawn to the river. On candelabra-lit sideboards, her servants placed trays heaped with pineapples, grapes, almonds, and raisins, along with decanters of port, sherry, and claret. The men, after gaining permission from the ladies, lighted Cuban torpedo cigars.

As if in an effort to rescue the faltering dinner table discussion, Mrs. Willabelle turned to Jessie and remarked, "I'm so sorry your companion, Mr. Ki, couldn't be here tonight with you. I gather he left quite hurriedly on one of your steamboats for Estero."

Before Jessie could respond, Senator Brockett let out a short laugh and added, "With that fellow aboard, Indianhead will have a lot less problem keeping those river riffraffs at bay."

But Jessie didn't commit herself. "Ki can always be counted on to give the best," she said evasively and changed the subject. "Indianhead is looked forward to a very good year, actually. This is great wheat country. Didn't I understand at dinner that you've planted thousands of acres, Mrs. Willabelle, and expect a high yield?"

"Oh, my, it's not really any of my doing," Mrs. Willabelle replied modestly. "My late husband studied wheat for years, you see, even way back when it was considered insane to

16

invest in ploughs and machinery and barbed wire to keep out livestock. He knew soil and he knew seed. I'm reaping the benefits, that's all."

Another man, puffing on his cigar, commented, "Only one thing could ruin a bumper crop now. Early rains. Doubtful, I'd say."

"It's getting a bit smoky in here. I believe we might do with some air," said Mrs. Willabelle, who went over and pulled back a set of heavy drapes, then unlatched a French door and swung it wide. Through the open doorway could be heard the sounds of a riverboat, the clatter of a passing buggy, and the neigh of a horse. Returning, Mrs. Willabelle seemed intent on making one more try for information, for she asked Jessie, "Will you be leaving soon for Estero, too?"

Again Jessie hedged. "Well, it's certainly true that the San Joaquin River has been the main target area for attacks on Indianhead shipping. So I imagine I may go to Estero, if I feel it would help, but I'm not sure exactly when that'd be."

"Surely after my gala," Brockett interjected hopefully.

"I sympathize with you, Miss Starbuck. As you doubtlessly know, I've enough acreage owned and under contract to support a barge line of my own," Mrs. Willabelle continued, "and it was raided a short time ago in the delta. Everything demolished and several men killed. Do you have any idea what's behind it all?"

"It's one way to drive out competition," Jessie said dryly.

Brockett raised his eyebrows in surprise. "Are you sure?"

"No proof." Jessie shook her head. "But you must admit it's having that effect. Understand, I'm talking in confidence and not accusing anyone."

"Definitely. You can say what you like here."

"I'm saying nothing yet, Mrs. Willabelle. I'm only asking for help. You're the largest landowner from Marysville

17

to Fresno, and you're a local resident with extensive contacts. I've heard it said that you know every company and person in the county."

"I try to keep up with things," the elderly widow simpered. "I'll do all I can to help, but after all, I'm only a woman. And I must confess, I mostly dabble in the business here. My late husband's home office in Paris handles most of the matters."

That startled Jessie. "You're French-owned?"

Mrs. Willabelle laughed. "No, not really. My husband was French, his initial stake came from there, so he kept his company base there, and I've seen no reason to change it, especially considering our many European interests. But that's not the point now. I'll do what I can and will pass on any information that comes my way, particularly about any unscrupulous competitors."

Throughout this brief conversation, Jessie had been standing tensely, a tingle of alarm running through her senses. She watched cautiously, her ears straining for any foreign sound, still feeling an aura of danger in the air. There were noises from the river. the laughter of a boy and girl as they passed nearby.

Few would have heard the next sound, but it carried to Jessie's sensitive ears. Most of her life had been spent where death was only a whisper, only a breath away. Now her trained ears caught the faint click of a revolver coming to full cock.

Instantly she dived sideward, a shout of warning on her lips. The sweep of her arm sent the candelabrum nearest her crashing to the floor. A revolver blasted and its muzzle flame made a bright streak at the open doorway. Not caring how she looked, but caring how she lived, Jessie rolled across the carpet, tugging open her tiny purse and grasping for her derringer. She heard the harsh plunk as the bullet from the ambusher's weapon burrowed into the heavy sideboard. Some of the women were screaming, the men were shouting, and Senator Brockett was calling for her to take care.

Instead Jessie took aim. Hardly had the gun flash died at the doorway than her stubby pistol blazed a response. She triggered twice, as fast as she could, the sharp discharges not drowning out the hoarse scream outside the doorway.

"You got him!" Brockett yelled.

In a display of bravado—or rashness—Mrs. Willabelle's butler had flung open the room's side door and disappeared into the night. Then Jessie was on her feet. Just as she and Brockett reached the doorway, she heard the report of three more quickly fired shots. Rushing out into the warm night air, she saw the butler standing over a huddled form on the ground, gripping a revolver—an uncommon type, Jessie noted peripherally, an Austrian Roth-Gasser, chambered for a unique 11.2mm black powder cartridge. With Brockett and a couple of other men at her heels, Jessie moved toward the butler, who turned to them.

"I got him!" he announced. "You shots winged him, Miss Starbuck, but I finished him off. Trying to kill a guest in Madam's own house!" There seemed to be genuine anger in his voice.

Now the rest of the party was gathering around, including Mrs. Willabelle, who came carrying another, still-lit candelabrum. She held it over the body on the ground, not turning so much as a hair at the grisly sight, but staring down with an expression of outrage, disgust, and surprise. Jessie also gazed at the dead scarred face, trying to recall if she'd ever seen him before.

She had not. Nor, when she asked, did anyone else recognize the dead man. Brockett knelt and quickly rifled through his pockets, but found nothing except some loose money, a pouch of tobacco and papers, and a battered silver watch.

"Oh me, oh my, how will I ever live this down?" Mrs. Willabelle sighed to herself, then smiled vast relief at Jessica. "I'm so thankful this wretched brute missed you, missed all of us, and that you came so, ah . . . well prepared for emergencies."

Jessie nodded, thinking wryly that Mrs. Willabelle had nothing to live down, but would be the social toast of the season because of this botched ambush. As for herself, she reloaded her derringer and replaced it in her purse, commenting, "Yes, it was close."

For several minutes everyone searched the ground for tracks. It was futile, the grass dry and the earth hard after a long hot summer. When the butler reported that no sign of the gunman's horse, or of any other means of his arrival, could be found, Jessie shrugged and faced Mrs. Willabelle's head servant.

"Thank you for saving my life, Mr.—uh?"

"Hubert, and no mister about it. Just Hubert, at your service, Miss Starbuck." The butler didn't bow or lower his gaze in false servility, but eyed her squarely, cool and calm. "I didn't save you. You saved you, but we both got him."

The bloody incident had cast a pall over the dinner party and quashed any real desire for it to continue. By the time the police had come and gone with the body, everyone was ready to bid his regretful respects and leave. Jessie was about to have a carriage summoned for her, but Senator Brockett insisted she allow him to escort her back to her hotel.

"You absolutely must accompany me," he told her forcefully. "No telling if there are other fiends out hoping to catch you alone."

Jessie hesitated a polite moment, then gratefully accepted

20

his offer. She wasn't afraid of going back by herself nor did she doubt her ability to defend herself, yet there was always a chance of confronting odds too strong and deadly for one person to handle. Besides, she had questions she wanted to ask him. And she liked the man; she always found him, on her infrequent visits here, to be gracious and outgoing and deeply concerned with the welfare of his constituents. Not that she had any fooling around in mind, she thought hastily. After the food and liquor and her close brush with death, her only desire now was to go to bed. Alone. To sleep.

Shortly, Jessica was seated demurely beside Brockett on the green plush bench of his quarter-top buggy, heading toward central Sacramento and the Grand Union Hotel. The stars were low in the moonlit sky, making a brilliant pattern in the heavens. It was hard to realize that a bullet had almost claimed her life.

"What's your opinion of Mrs. Willabelle?" she asked him.

Brockett shrugged. "Richer'n sin and as powerful. She's tougher than she likes to talk, too. But she's well-liked by most people she meets, I believe, and I haven't heard anything against her. Why?"

"Nothing special. I was just wondering why her butler had to kill a man already down. It's not unknown for crooks to do that, to keep henchmen from talking if anything goes wrong."

"I doubt that's the case," Brockett responded, chuckling. "Hubert is dedicated and loyal, but not the most intelligent man, and he was most likely too keyed up and irate and shot reflexively."

"You're probably right. Forget I even mentioned it."

"In answer to your next question, Jessie, I checked into the state-recorded manifests and declarations, as you wanted me to. I located where four tons of government-surplus guns and ammunition were sold at auction several months ago

21

and were shipped from the Baltimore arsenal 'round the Horn and to Sacramento."

Jessie tensed, staring into the senator's grave face. "Four tons is enough to start a small war! Who bought them?"

"A certain Fenton Chadwick. He cuts quite a figure down Estero way, so I hear tell—a big, influential farmer who's currently running for a seat on the Merced County Board of Commissioners. A law-and-order man, who's going to stamp out crime if it kills him."

"Or so he campaigns?"

"Yep. I personally don't care for him much, but, like Mrs. Willabelle, I don't know of any skunks roped to his coattails. Anyhow, I assume the arms and ammo were transferred down to him."

Jessie lapsed quiet, mulling over Brockett's ominous news.

They rolled into the central district, which was as lively by night as by day, for there were as many saloons and gaming halls as there were respectable businesses. Men came in after dark from the nearby hills where claims were still being worked. And, with Sacramento a river town through which freight passed to and from the back country, there were many teamsters, dock-wallopers, and common laborers about each night. Batwing doors swung busily.

The Pickax, directly across from the hotel on Second and J Streets, was the biggest, rowdiest bar. Its spot was not only incongruous because the Grand Union was the poshest and snootiest hotel in town, but also because of the adjacent B. F. Hastings Building, where the the most august and prestigious tenants had offices—including Wells Fargo, the California Supreme Court, and, naturally, Indianhead Marine Transportation Company.

Reining in by the front of the hotel, Brockett extended his hand and Jessie grasped it firmly. Their eyes met.

"Thanks, Charles, and I'm afraid good-bye, too," she

said, stepping down. "I can't come to your reception. Too much to do."

"I understand. Be careful, Jessie, I've a feeling—"

The senator's parting was interrupted by a sudden uproar across at the saloon. A huge, bearded man in the rough garb of a miner came half reeling, half bowling out the door, followed by a raucous surge of hooting and swearing from those inside. He landed akilter in a horse trough, rear end upright, shook himself the way a dog might after getting soaked, and plunged back in, his face contorted by his night's bout.

"That does it," Brockett declared, swinging down. "I'm not taking any chances, Jessie, I'll see you to your room."

"My . . . room?"

"And I'll check it inside, too, just to be on the safe side."

Grasping her by the arm, he propelled her into the hotel lobby. The manager stepped forward to greet Jessie deferentially, but hastily turned aside as they swept past him. A single man taking a single lady to her room would normally have resulted in the manager's giving them the bum's rush, but considering who these two were, well . . . Better a blind eye than a hotel scandal.

After a fast moment at the desk to collect her room key, they trooped upstairs to Jessie's suite. Jessie wanted to protest, but in much the same manner as the manager, figured that to make a public fuss here would be worse than to go quickly and quietly.

Brockett unlocked the door to her room and went in first. Soft lamplight radiated across the large rectangular room, the bulk of which was taken up by a monstrous canopied bed. Full-length brocade drapes tumbled casually on a thick carpet inside the many windows. Brockett checked behind the drapes, then the adjoining bathroom, and returned.

"Well, I'd say you're safe now, Jessie."

23

Jessie smiled up at him, admiring his husky torso, sun-tanned face, and vivid eyes. "Oh, I'm not so sure of that."

Brockett stepped closer, almost touching her. "Not sure?"

"That I'm safe now, Charles, not with you here."

"And the door closed." He chuckled, leaning. "You're not."

"Charles? Charles, what're you doing?"

What he was doing was kissing her, bending down and brushing his lips across her mouth. "You're a tease, you know."

"Well, this tease is tired." Her voice was soft, but her mouth was firm as she felt his pressing caress. "Stop it."

"I've wanted to do that," he said grinning.

She shook her head. "Don't say that, please don't."

"It's true. I didn't know it until now, but that's why I'm here, because I've wanted to kiss you ever since we first met." He breathed into her ear as he kissed her soft throat. "I watched you show off every time you came to town and damn near died from wanting you, Jessie. I still want you, more'n ever."

"I never showed myself off," she protested.

His chuckle teased her earlobe. "No? M'dear, the way you walk—strut—with such fey abandon. Your shirts haven't ever been thick enough to hide, much less hold in, your breasts. I watched them bobbing up and down, I heard those nipples rubbing the cloth, day after day. Ah, Lord! You're a tease, too much of a tease."

"No, no," she whispered intently, trying to maintain some semblance of decorum. His lips pulsed against hers again, and she sensed a perverse response, and intriguing tingle worming up through her flesh. She fought against it, turning rigid when he put his arms around her . . . and yet she allowed him to pull her in an embrace, and remained pliant in his arms, though not responding.

"Jessie . . ."

"No, Charles. Please go."

"Are you afraid?"

"I'm tired, I told you."

"I'll wake you up."

"That's what I'm afraid of." And it was the truth, for she felt this to be wrong. Not the kissing, nor the passion it was involuntarily igniting within her. She'd kissed and been passionate before. The wrongness was in the time and the place, and her fear that to continue might ruin the good working relationship they had together, which was based on respect and a sense of equality.

Yet, she was also oddly aware that there was more to this than mere kissing and passion. She knew the hard, harsh demands of a hungry body and she was strong enough to resist pure lust. What she was having a difficult time defying was the inexplicable flowing gentleness. His lips on hers, his tongue hot and pointed, touching her flattened lips, tasting the wetness of her parted mouth, seemed to suck the resistance from her, weaken her, leave her fluttering like an autumn leaf in the wind.

She leaned against him and accepted his kiss without really returning it, merely allowing it, letting him take her mouth, permitting her weak body to press his solid chest, feeling his arms firm against her sides as his hands touched and pressed in return. His was a touch of affection, of questioning exploration, and she could feel his heart. It pounded against her breast and she could feel its beat through the layers of their clothing. Her own heart was pounding, and, almost forelornly, she realized in that electric moment that she no longer felt tired at all.

"Don't, Jessie," he murmured. "Don't fight it."

"Charles, we can't—" She was trying to tell him he didn't know what he was saying, that they couldn't complete what he was starting, but his lips stopped her words and, for a moment, she lost herself in the kiss. The tip of her tongue touched his, and she felt a great, convulsive shiver go through him and it melted her. Her arms, possessing will of their own, went around him, felt the muscles tensed in his back, felt the masculine bulk of his body, and tightened in a quick, reflexive movement.

Then it was too late. She let her tongue flick against his in his mouth, and the glow of desire was strong in her. The wet mingling made her forget. They were just two people, a man and a woman kissing in a private room, preparing to make love. And with that confession, the last of her reserve drained away. She wanted him. God, how she wanted him!

"You have too many clothes on," he breathed.

His hands went to the snaps and clips of her gown, began undoing them. Down came the fabric to her waist, and Brockett smiled, staring at her breasts where they thrust against her chemise, the sheer cambric material like a white mist over her dark, jutting nipples. He eased the chemise down off her shoulders, baring her breasts, his fingers brushing the nipples.

"By God, you've got gorgeous breasts!" he exclaimed.

His palms cupped her full, taut globes, lifting them. He moved them gently, up and down, then removed his hands and bent to kiss each nipple hungrily. He was starting to pant, nursing on her, his hands caressing her naked sides, kindling a fire in her loins. It had been awhile for her, and she too was hungry.

She moaned again, her head moving back and forth.

"Me, Jessie . . . me!" he gasped.

Her hands went to his belt buckle, unclasped it. She was a little out of her head from weariness, from the arousal of her flesh, and felt somewhat like a slave girl attending her master. Her fingers unbuttoned his fly, reached in, her fingers tender and gentle as she stroked his hardened male girth. Then, drawing his erection out into the open, she drew back to admire him as he had admired her breasts. His manhood was absolutely bounteous.

Eager now, Jessie moved her hands to his breeches and pushed them down. Brockett didn't make it any easier, for he had his big hands under her breasts while she leaned to take his pants all the way to his ankles, and he so tickling her as to make her near die of delight. And he was not only big; he was wildly aroused.

"We still have too many clothes on," he groaned.

The broke free of each other, unable to wait, and began stripping hurriedly. Jessie bent, gripping the hem of her gown and chemise, yanking them upward over her head and off. Brockett was in a frenzy, tossing his suit jacket, pants, shirt, and shoes, and Jessie watched him strip as she peeled off her drawstring drawers. He was muscular, a little fat about the middle where he was developing a paunch from too much good food and drink, but his chest was still strong and hirsute, and his thick member was virile and raring to go.

When his underwear was on the floor, he moved forward to plaster his naked self against her naked self. They rubbed fronts for a time, while his mouth again feasted on her lips and his hands played around her buttocks and upper thighs. His hard spearing organ teased against her until Jessie was gasping and crying, her nerve ends on fire as his erection brushed back and forth over her sensitive female portal.

Then he was raising her up, widening her thighs, crouching as he assumed the male position of entry. A part of Jessie turned inside out, and lurched forward and downward, mewling. Brockett chuckled at her erotic eagerness, slowly sliding between her flushed thighs, driving inward, burrowing deep and still deeper, steadily. Jessie was only vaguely aware that he was gripping her on either side of her naked hips, that he was letting her loins do all the work while he merely crouched supporting her.

27

She could not control her reactions. With his feet between her legs, with her feet planted on his legs, and with his palms beneath her buttocks, she rode his shaft up and down. Slowly he walked her to the bed, while she continued to dance and jerk on him, unable to breath, her throat tight with the needs of her body.

Gently he lowered her till she was supine on the coverlet, even as she kept on hammering against him, sweat trickling down her face and dripping from her bobbing breasts. He nearly withdrew as he tried to maintain his balance, and she twisted and writhed, stifling the lurid impulse to plead for more. She knew instinctively there would be more, much more, for it was obvious that Brockett knew his way about female anatomy and was greedy to show her how well he knew.

Then, repositioned above her, Brockett plunged fully inside. She placed both hands on his buttocks and urged him still deeper, her lips burning against his again, forming moaning sounds without meaning. He shoved his hips forward, forcing her bottom to grind against the bed, forcing his turgid member to fill her aching inner depths. Her pointed nipples stabbed his chest at each new thrust of their loins. Her lips continued to shape sweet, worldless sighs in rhythm to his plunging tempo. Her knees bent higher, her ankles climbing his back, allowing him to penetrate more fully. Her ankle-lock persisted until their combined weight was on the small of her arching back, and her calves were almost tucked under his armpits.

Jessie's murmurings began to change in tone and pitch, and both of them realized she was building to her climax. Yet she had not started to climax in earnest; there was still time, she still wanted more. Sensing her unleashed yearnings, Brockett levered himself up, let her place her legs above his shoulders, then shoved home once again, swiftly and savagely. In unison they pumped faster and faster, Jessie virtually bent double, her eyes dilated, mouth twisted, muttering incoherently.

She felt the senator's answering throbs and knew he was rapidly spiraling toward his own release. She felt her own loins quivering on the verge of orgasm and strove harder, faster, to grip him with her moist, moving sheath. Intolerable pressure rose in her belly, even as Brockett's rampaging erection erupted deep inside her thirsty flesh.

"Yesss" she hissed, shivering, gritting her teeth, and clenching her eyes closed as her own climax overwhelmed her. Her legs extended toward the canopy as her seething loins held ravenously the torrent flooding into her . . . and then they splayed wide and dropped limply on either side of Brockett.

Brockett fell forward, remaining locked between her pulsating thighs. Finally, after a long sigh of contentment, he withdrew, rolling onto his side and propping himself on one elbow to gaze at her, smiling. Her eyes met his while she lay in quivering satiation, her flesh drained of energy, yet sensually alive.

"Never have I known a woman like you," he murmured.

Jessie laughed softly and embraced him. They lay like that for quite some while, until, tentatively, his lips began kissing her throat, and he started showing signs of renewed strength. There was a madness in their flesh, even though they were pretty exhausted by this time.

For hours they continued to enjoy each other, their inventiveness equalled only by the desire surging through their flesh. Her hands caressed his body. They kissed. His teeth nipped her buttocks, her nipples, her dewy inner thighs.

Sometime in the wee hours, they slept.

Sometime toward dawn, Brockett rolled from her bed, dressed, and quietly departed. She didn't know when, but sensed the loss.

Chapter 3

In the flush of a serene, fiery dawn, Jessica began her long overland trek to Gunther Mellon's farm, outside Estero. She was full from an excellent hotel breakfast, feeling pleasantly sore between her thighs, and was riding a reasonably good roan gelding rented from a nearby livery stable. Man-style, she rode, not so-called "lady-like" on a torturous side-saddle perch; and she was clad in her figure-squeezing denim jeans and jacket. Her derringer lay concealed behind the wide square buckle of her belt with her cartridge belt and holster looped over the horn of her rental stock saddle, so that her custom .38 Colt revolver wouldn't chafe her thigh.

Tied to the saddle apron was her leather-bound canvas telescope bag, pliable enough not to gouge the horse carrying it, yet expandable enough to contain her necessities. And while she rode, Jessie mulled over the small black notebook which she kept in that bag, and which she had carefully studied over breakfast.

Contained within the notebook's covers was a ledger detailing the names and activities of a vicious international ring intent upon gaining control of America's business and political establishment. Jessie's father had started compiling the information while in the Orient, during his first meager years of building what would ultimately become the Starbuck business empire, and he had scrupulously kept the book up to date ever since. In his subsequent battles with this criminal conspiracy, his wife was killed while Jessie was yet a babe. Alex Starbuck avenged that murder, but eventually he, too, fell victim to the cartel. By then, however, Jessie was a young woman, old enough to know and to understand his persistent fight, and she, in turn, avenged his death.

The book which Jessie now carried was a copy of her father's original notebook, which she kept under lock and key back at her Circle Star Ranch. Jessie had continued to add to and update its entries, some through her personal experience, and others from reports compiled by the same private detectives who'd worked for her father. By using these secret records and her powerful inheritance, and aided by Ki, Jessie had been struggling on against the deadly cartel, as determined as her father had been to destroy it utterly.

Up till last night, there'd been no indication that the troubles plaguing Indianhead involved the cartel. The sneak attack at the party, though, had set Jessie to wondering— not so much the attack itself, as the facts that Mrs. Willabelle's operations were headquartered in Europe and that her butler had a name that was possibly German and had used an Austrian-made pistol. And the cartel, although worldwide in scope, was European based and of Prussion origin.

Nothing in the notebook, however, showed any linkage. Nobody appeared listed by name or description, not even the late Mr. Willabelle's company in Paris; and God only knew how many Austrian weapons and men named Hubert— which, ironically, was Teutonic for "Bright minded"—were to be found on both continents. Still, it was something to consider, to keep in mind. And Jessie did.

For the first few hours, Jessie beat south by southwest, the main wagon road angling toward the gold camp towns that strung along the Sierra foothills. The road then curved southward to connect with Fresno, and all along its route there were many secondary trails heading east and west to various communities.

By mid-morning Jessie was at the junction of the main road and the trail leading to Estero. She paused at the junction's way station for a quick meal, this being the last spot for food before she reached the Mellon farm; and because the day had become so hot by then, she removed her jacket in favor of her cotton shirt.

There was a short yet harsh stretch of foothills between here and the San Joaquin Valley, and the trail kept close to its rugged contours, rarely crossing along the ridges, but squirreling through clefts and hollows. Then the trail began narrowing, and soon she climbed to the beginning of a ledge passage. Granite walls went up, hot and crumbly, for a hundred feet above the trail, while on the other side was a longer drop into the gorge of an unnamed, cascading stream.

Her rented roan was no thoroughbred racer, but it was sure-footed as a goat and took the trail cautiously, stepping lightly. For two hundred yards they followed the trail around the face of the rock wall and came upon a jut of stone, cutting off view ahead and narrowing the way even further— and it was then that she heard the ring of shod hooves somewhere beyond.

Jessie frowned. She had hardly expected this minor trail to be so heavily used, and as she glanced back along the path she had come, she saw that backtracking with an unfamiliar horse would present a ticklish problem. Warily she jigged the roan on.

Just beyond the stone bulge, the ledge trail cut sharply in against the cliff face where some ancient fall had left a wider shelf rock. It was thirty yards to the shelf, and half that distance to the bulge which blotted out the trail directly ahead.

"C'mon, boy," she urged her horse. "Let's make that wide spot in the trail before whoever is up ahead of us does."

She didn't make it. A burly man rounded the rock bulge,

riding a tired gray mare. He saw Jessie and pulled up short, facing her across sixty feet of sheer space. A slim, sallow-faced man showed up behind him, riding a nervous bay.

The slim man said, "Well, well, I tol' you we had company behind us, Bremmer. I tol' you I heard someone."

The broad man scowled and then grinned craftily. He quickened his pace, made the wide point in the trail, and waited for his companion to join him. The sweat on his forehead glistened in the sun, and he daubed his brow with a dirty sleeve, while licking perspiration from around his lips. He wore two pistols, while his companion was armed with only one, a nut-handled Smith & Wesson .44. But to Jessie's experienced eye, she judged the sallow-faced man to be the more dangerous in a fight.

She considered the situation. There was enough room at the shelf to allow her passage, if both men and animals squeezed in against the cliff. She gave a light tug to her reins and started forward again.

"What's your hurry, honey?" the burly man sneered.

Jessie stiffened. "My husband's waiting just up ahead," she retorted coldly. "I'm bringing him his lunch from the waystation."

"That's odd. We didn't pass nobody on our way here," the man said, again licking lips like slices of liver. Jessie knew that was as much a lie as hers; his companion had already mentioned having heard someone behind them, meaning they must've been heading in the same direction as she, rather than having been traveling toward her. They'd doubled back to check, but why?

The man's companion shook his head disgustedly. "C'mon, Bremmer. Leave a lady be for once. We got places to get to."

But Bremmer's eyes were glittering hungrily. "Take it easy. We've made good time, and no tellin' what else we can make if we put our mind to it, Milo." He turned to Jessie again, leering. "Besides, we're here first, so's anyone backing, it's gonna be you."

Jessie shook her head. "It's better than two hundred yards behind him, and my horse would have to back all the way. I think I can get past you there, if you'll crowd your mounts to the wall."

Bremmer's eyes widened in mock surprise. "Well, hear the honey, Milo. She's telling us she wants to squeeze in with us." He laughed with an ugly, throaty sound. "Come on, honey. Say what's your name, and whatcha doin' way out here?"

Jessie, seeing that appealing to their decency would be a waste of breath, tried a different tack. She smiled shyly and folded her hands on her pommel, around which her cartridge belt and holster were looped, hidden from the men, and she said, "Verna's my name. And like I said, my husband—"

"Sure, sure, honey. And what he don't know, won't hurt you."

"Gee, if I *did* do something with you that he wouldn't know about, how'd I know you wouldn't just kill me afterwards?"

Now even Milo was perking up. "Hell, nothin' so crude. We'd be all so grateful, we'd leave you with mayhaps a little pin money."

Believe that! Jessie acted like she did. "Well . . . I can't take you handsome guys on both at once, y'know. Who's first?"

Milo said to Brenner, "Let's toss for dibbies. Heads."

"Awrigh'," Bremmer drawled, scrounging in his pocket for a coin. The glint in his eye warned Jessie—and most likely Milo—that he had no intention of abiding by the toss. He flicked the coin into the air, caught it, and opened his palm.

"Tails," he announced. "I win, Milo."

Milo said, "Lemme see," and put out his hand.

And Jessie, figuring their distraction was her first and probably only chance, drew her revolver. Milo, with a startled oath, glimpsed her action and stabbed for his .44. He was fast, as fast as Jessie had feared he'd be, but Jessie was already leveling her Colt when Milo was still bringing up his pistol.

Smoke wreathed Jessie's hip. Her first slug ripped Milo's pistol from his grip; the second smashed the sallow man's arm. Milo made a grab for his saddlehorn with his good hand, as his bay, spooked by the shots, crowded into Bremmer's mare. It threw off Bremmer's slower draw and allowed Jessie a moment to heel her roan forward. There was a snorting tangle of horses, then the bay lost its footing and fell backward off the trail.

Milo gave out one short, horrible scream. Bremmer, ignoring his partner, was intent on swinging his drawn weapon on Jessie and blasting her pointblank in the stomach. Jessie couldn't respond in time with her Colt. She had purposely wedged her roan forward between the rock wall and the men, and there was so little room to maneuver, and the roan was fishing so nervously, that her gunarm was momentarily stuck against the stone.

Desperate, Jessie closed her free hand on Bremmer's hairy wrist. She yanked downward, deflecting his pistol, and as the startled man lurched sideway, Jessie shouldered him as hard as she could. The impact toppled Bremmer the other way, and losing his balance, he unseated himself, boots slipping from stirrups, and dove tumbling off his horse and down into the gorge.

Milo had screamed as he fell. Bremmer dropped without a sound.

For seconds after the abrupt set-to, Jessie sat still, a thin dribble of smoke issuing from her Colt. On the trail beside her, the gray mare was still quivering. A shadow floated

35

down from the opposite wall of the gorge, dipping toward the ledge trail, then made a wide, climbing circle into the sky. It was joined by another, and the two scavenger hawks dropped in long, ominous glides for the canyon bottom.

Jessie slowly holstered her revolver. She had killed again. But if they hadn't insisted on making a fight of it, they wouldn't have died. She'd have forced them to shuck their clothes down to their underwear, then taken their clothes and horses up ahead—just to make sure they didn't go after her or anyplace else too fast—but at least they'd still have been alive. She had only a minute or so to spare for remorse; that's all the likes of men like them were worth, and anyway, there was a distance for her yet to go.

She heeled her roan to the wide shelf, having a delicate moment prompting the horse past the still nervous mare. The mare shied once they were by and trotted off along the trail behind her, fully capable, Jessie was sure, of fending for itself. Beyond the blind curve, the stone bulge ended in a broad, shallow-sloped hillside of boulders and scrub. The trail left the gorge at this point and wound around the hillside, then began descending gradually through broken, brush-clogged uplands toward the San Joaquin Valley.

Jessie was just entering the bend when a voice in back of her called sharply: "So you downed them! Set quiet, and keep your hand away from that gun of yours, or I'll drill you. I can't miss!"

Reining sharply and freezing, her back exposed to a leveled weapon, Jessie tried to see her foe from the corner of her eye. But the person—a woman by the sound of her feminine voice—was too well concealed by the hillside's shoulder, where some large rocks had fallen to form one side of the cut.

She glanced ruefully at where her revolver dangled against the roan's flank, and, as the silence grew unbearable, she said loudly, "I'm not a statue. What do you want me to do?"

"Don't be impatient. I'm sort of surprised myself."

It was a good sign, the woman being willing to talk. It gave Jessie time, and she sought for a way to glimpse the woman, who sounded cautious, determined, and somewhat sardonic.

She heard hoofsteps and the rattle of gravel and surmised the woman was easing a horse down to the trail from where she'd been hiding among the boulders. "Turn around slowly," the woman said. "I want to see the face that sent those fellows to hell."

Now, as Jessie complied, she saw a woman astride a scarred dun. She was wearing a corduroy blouse, a split skirt of melton wool, and a wraparound cloak of some other stout but well-worn material. She was about forty, Jessie estimated, but she could have been less; whatever her years, they'd been lived hard, the cold, revealing light of day treating her less kindly than the soft yellow glow of bar and boudoir lamps. She had sherry-colored hair and bee-stung lips that were very red against the pallor of her face. She stared at Jessie with eyes as hard and dark as whiskey bottle glass and held steady aim with a nickel-plated Banker's Special pistol.

"Hmm, you're better'n average," the woman observed. "I can see why Bremmer and Milo went for you, pawin' and bellerin'."

"They went for me, all right. You heard it?"

"Oh, yes, I heard it all. Couldn't see it, though. Milo fetched me up in those rocks while he and Bremmer went back after whoever was dogging them. I suppose that was you. Why were you?"

"I wasn't. I simply happened along the same trail," Jessie answered firmly. "I wasn't after them, in any form."

"Can't blame you much. Bremmer's got a body odor that'd make a skunk gag. But there're worst fates. When you get to my age and still have your hair to curl, you'll understand it. If you don't, well, that'll be that."

Jessica sat unresponsive and waited.

The woman then said, "Don't look snippy at me. We're all people, even if we got different ways of livin' and lovin'. That's my sermon. How far is Estero from here, Verna? It's Verna, right?"

"That's what I told them," Jessie confirmed and purposely grew more amiable. "Estero's the rest of the day's ride. I'm on my way there—or was, till y'all stopped me for tea."

Her jest brought a mild chuckle. "Maybe Mr. Chadwick will have you in for a drink when we get there. I dunno, though. I don't think he'll want to thank you much for what you did."

Jessie, throttling her surprise at hearing the name, picked it up as a cue. "So you're planning to see Fenton, are you? Bless me, then we must be friends on account I'm very *close* friends with Fenton, if you know what I mean."

"I know," the woman said, and she laughed out loud, Jessie having amused her. "Lawd, if only Bremmer and Milo had known! Oh, that's rich, that's rich!"

"Tell you what, why don't we ride together?"

"Sure, Verna, why not. On the way we can chew the breeze a little. Tell the truth, I just hate to ride alone."

The woman, smiling, lowered her pistol and took it off cock. But she didn't put the weapon completely away, nor did she avert her attention from Jessie as, riding on the left and slightly behind, she set her horse trotting with Jessie's along the trail.

Her talk, though, remained genial and lively, her voice liquor raspy and loud. "Names are sometimes funny, aren't they? Mine starts with *V*, just like yours does. Virginia, Virginia Arps, it is, but the fellows insist on calling me Va-ginie, I don't know why."

Jessie smiled, as Virginia Arps slapped her thigh and

38

laughed. Jessie might have run for it then, but that wasn't the way she wanted to play just yet. She resented Virginia's breezy familiarity, the close call she had had with the crude woman. Virginia, much less the two men who'd evidently been escorting her, had definitely thrown a wrench into her travel plans. Now Jessie was committed as a lover of Fenton Chadwick, and the instant they met the man Virginia would discover she was not even known by him. Only the fact that Virginia was a stranger had saved Jessie from a death bullet . . . and Jessie wanted to know what had led to this dangerous impasse.

For some while, Virginia told ribald accounts and risqué jokes that were chestnuts back in the days of the Revolution. Yet all the while she never gave Jessie the slightest opportunity to gain an advantage. Jessie thought it was just natural shrewd caution, for Virginia seemed to accept her as a friend and one of Fenton Chadwick's group. Finally Jessie's silence, speaking only when directly questioned, began to irk the woman.

"You're a quiet young thing, aren't you?" she complained. "When I was your age, I was a hellcat on wheels. Thought of nothing but men and money. Now I think of nothing but money and men!"

That set Virginia off in another gale of cackling, but seeing it fail to gain much response from Jessie, she apparently sought to impress Jessie another way. For sobering, Virginia patted her blouse, and a paper rattle between her breasts.

"Mr. Chadwick will be mighty glad to see me, Verna. I'm bringing him word straight from the dragon in Sacramento."

"Oh, you're from Sacramento!" Jessie exclaimed. "Sure, Fenton will be pleased—and generous, I bet—that you've come. He's been expecting you."

"He has? How does he think I ride, on wings? I was sent

39

out the day his message reached that ol' battleax. Me an' the fellows made real fast time, too, considerin' the stops."

Jessie had a fair notion what sort of stops had been taken, but had no idea who "the dragon" and "that old battleax" might be. She desperately wished she did, but to ask Virginia would be tantamount to admitting her masquerade. Virginia wasn't dumb, even if she was a crass, unpleasant harridan. The lewd banter was a bore and covered a calculating, cruel nature that was entirely self-centered. Virginia was a dangerous opponent.

"So you know Fenton," Jessie replied blithely.

"Who, me? No, never met him, though I've heard enough. The way things are going with these farmboys kicking up their clodhoppin' heels we gotta stick together. Agreed?"

"Agreed. But there's a tough bunch of nuts in these parts."

"Your Chadwick with our fellows will crack 'em wide open," Virginia declared. "We're all in this together, aren't we?"

"To the death," Jessie affirmed stoutly, without adding whose death she had in mind. Inwardly she ached to get the better of Virginia before too much longer. Fenton Chadwick was expecting a messenger from a partner or employer, but in any case a powerful ally, up in Sacramento. The woman was being used to relay it, which, Jessie perceived, was a pretty cagey method of delivery. Certainly the use of women as couriers was one that would fool all but the most suspicious. But Virginia remained suspicious of Jessie, if only out of habit, and was never off guard.

They rode down out of the foothills into the huge bowl of the San Joaquin Valley, and as they came to the great fields, Virginia was astonished at the endless, waving wheat.

"What's all this?" she asked. "Wheat, isn't it?"

"That's right."

They continued along the fenced fields that hemmed both sides of the trail, Virginia studying the man-tall grain bowing softly in the hot summer zephers. "Awful lot of it. Must be worth a lot of money these days. Folks gotta eat, don't they?"

Jessie nodded.

"Pull in and let's take a closer look," Virginia said.

"We really should be pushing along, if we're to reach—"

"Pull in, I said." Virginia demanded, her voice no longer friendly. The click of her pistol hammer's being cocked emphasized her order. "Pull in and get down. We'll walk from here."

Tensing, Jessie reined in and slowly dismounted. "Easy now, Virginia. No call to get upset. I was just thinking—"

"Thinkin' too damn much, if you ask me," Virginia cut in brutally and gestured with her pistol. "Crawl through that fence and start walking into that there field, Miss Starbuck."

"What? No, I'm Ver—"

"I knew you were the Starbuck gal from the start." Virginia, dismounting, stepped closer. "You never once tricked me with your phony name and ways. I tricked you instead!"

Jessie smiled softly and lowered her arms. "I confess, Virginia, you got me. Just trying to be foxy, is all, only you sure are foxier. Tell me, seeing as you got the drop on me, why'd you wait till now? And how'd you know who I am?"

"I got more'n one piece of paper on me. I got a picture drawn of you with a reward for proving you're dead. I'll give 'em proof—one of your ears." The woman's face contorted in a derisive snarl. "But I couldn't dump you just any ol' place, where you'd be found easily. The wheat'll hide you for a long time."

Obviously Virginia had no idea of this being the reaping

season and that a body in a field would soon be discovered. But that was of little consolation to Jessie. She hooked her thumbs on her belt buckle and sighed, clucking her tongue. "No, I don't believe I'll walk into that field and let you kill me."

"Then I'll shoot you here and carry you in."

"Let's work something else out. If it's money—"

"It's satisfaction, too." Virginia stepped back a pace. "Thinkin', always thinkin' you're better'n us plain folk."

The bullet entered her lower chest while she was still talking. It hit straight, shot from Jessie's derringer when she snapped the hidden gun out from behind her belt buckle. The woman seemed paralyzed from the impact of the .38 slug, mouth wide as if to change her talking to screaming, but no sound coming out.

Jessie was in motion even as the bullet struck. She leaped for Virginia, snatching the pistol from her nerveless fingers, just before the woman slowly crumpled to sprawl inert, face down.

After a moment to make sure the woman was dead, Jessie rolled her over on her back. She found, as Virginia had bragged, two papers stuffed down between her lifeless breasts. One was a crude, privately printed "wanted" circular with a pen-and-ink portrait of Jessie and Ki, offering five hundred dollars for evidence of each's death. To be paid by whom or where was not spelled out.

The other was a letter in a white envelope, folded once. It was addressed to Fenton Chadwick, Estero, and it read:

Dear Fenwick:
Yrs rec'd. Have obtained similar to what you want and am arranging it to be forwarded promptly. Agree it is high time we cleaned up your section once and for all, so we can forge ahead with our chain through-

out the valley. Am sending thirty additional men with
your Big Surprise that will guarantee our victory. Yrs.

Like the wanted poster, the letter had no signature, no
imprint of its sender. The most Jessie could glean from it
was that whoever had written it had excellent penmanship.

Jessie slipped the papers into her breast pocket, then
turned her attention to Virginia's dead body. She was heavy
to lift and cumbersome to thrust over the barbed wire fence,
but Jessie finally managed to haul her body across and deep
into the wheat field, where it was unceremoniously depos-
ited, temporarily out of sight. It was, Jessie thought, a fitting
resting place for a while, considering that was the fate
Virginia had in mind for her. In a few days or weeks she'd
be found. Until then . . .

Returning to the trail, Jessie caught up with the woman's
horse, which was grazing nearby on wheat fronds sticking
over the barbed wire fence. She unsaddled the dun, then
went through Virginia's saddlebags, but found only food,
spare ammunition, and personal effects. She concealed the
gear and turned the dun loose.

Checking her appearance and weapons, Jessie set her
roan's head once again toward Estero and Gunther Mellon's
outlying farm. Virginia Arps had displayed a certain guile
and gut charm that might have led some otherwise smart
men down the garden path—and she had almost led Jessie
to her death. And while Jessie was saddened, she was not
about to carry futile regrets over that woman, or over
Bremmer and Milo. There was steel in her, tempered and
hardened by her hatred of lawlessness and unyielding demands of her battle against the cartel. There was no retreat
for her, nothing she would allow to turn her back. So she
closed her mind to the silent accusation of Virginia's death
and looked ahead.

And in looking ahead Jessie wondered anxiously what

43

sort of secret weapon was being shipped to Chadwick. Well, whatever it was, she was determined to fight against it and those using it with every trick and all the ruthlessness at her command, if the enemy made such methods necessary. And she would prevail.

Chapter 4

Jessie continued following the trail through the surrounding sea of wheat. As far as she could survey, the fields stretched heavy with grain, golden tips almost dazzling under the hot sun.

Barbed fences kept pace with her. They weren't massive or threatening, but were rigged just strong enough to discourage wandering livestock or horses, unless, of course, the animals were stampeding, in which case no fence would hold them. The fencing was evidently a community job, too, for the only divisions were made where other trails and private lanes cut into the vast expanses. And, as the day waned, Jessie also noted a few cattle grazing to the south and some smoke from a home that tinged the clean blue of the late afternoon sky to the west.

The shadows were long when she came to the fork leading to Estero. She chose it, unsure but figuring that along it somewhere should be the entrance to Mellon's property. Her guess was good, for shortly she spotted a wooden sign fastened to a stout logpole beside a wagon-rutted lane. The sign was professionally carved, not crude, and painted as the marker at the fork had been with the scrolled words *RANCHO MELLON* and a hand pointing down the lane.

Turning her horse onto the lane, she soon saw lamplit windows in a big, hacienda-style house that stood well in from the main trail on a low, rounded knoll directly ahead of her. By now the sun was slipping behind the Diablo

Mountains, which rimmed the western edge of the valley, and with dusk at hand, Jessie spurred her roan into a sprightly trot, eager to reach the house before dark.

Hoofbeats suddenly sounded nearby, and Jessie turned quickly, her hand dropping to her holster. A rider who had appeared out of a dry irrigation culvert was galloping toward her, gesturing for her to stop. She reined in and waited.

The rider, closing in alongside, was a swarthy, grim-faced man of about thirty with a solid medium build and utterly black hair and eyes. When he pulled up, he stared, scrutinizing her.

Jessie eyed him back. "I've come to see Gunther Mellon."

"Your name?" he demanded curtly.

"Miss Jessica Starbuck. If it comes to that, who're you?"

"I'm Tino Benedict, foreman here." He relaxed and grinned. "Oh yeah, your *segundo* arrived already, and I was told a lady of your name would be coming soon. C'mon, let me show you the way."

Benedict fell in on Jessie's left, and they fast-trotted along the lane easily. After a few moments the foreman cleared his throat and apologized. "Sorry about harassing you, Miss Starbuck. I really am glad to meet you." He slapped the stock of the carbine in his saddle-boot. "But, y'see, we're taking a close look at all strangers these days."

Jessie smiled slightly. "I gather you've had troubles."

"You gather right. Ours have been like yours with those river pirates, except if you ask me, our troubles are spelled Chadwick."

"How's he been bothering you?"

"I don't have proof. I'm speaking out of turn. But in my gut I'm sure Fenton Chadwick's *el diablo*—the devil—behind the raids and burnings that've been plaguing us. Eh, but you talk of it later, with Mr. Mellon. You must be tired and hungry."

Reaching the wide, bare yard fronting the house, they

rode toward it under a canopy of big, overhanging trees. Farmhands paused to stare at them, and several small boys—sons of the workers, Jessie presumed—stopped playing and scattered with giggling yells around the side of a harness shop.

The Mexican-influenced house stood at the far end of the yard's walled enclosure, half-hidden behind flower beds and small blooming shrubs. When they reined in by the front porch's hitchrail, Benedict remained asaddle and said to Jessie, "I'll leave you here, if you don't mind. You just go up and knock, okay?"

Jessie nodded and dismounted. "Is Ki inside?"

"No, he left shortly after noon to go to Estero." Benedict frowned, as if he didn't care to answer more questions.

So Jessie left it at that, except to add, "Thank you, Tino. By the way, Ki isn't my *segundo;* he's my close and personal friend."

"I'll remember that, Miss Starbuck, I sure will." Benedict called a man over to attend to Jessie's horse, then, with a parting nod, he swung off toward the bunkhouses and corral.

Jessie walked up on the porch and clanged the brass knocker that was attached to the middle of the front door. A well-dressed woman of Spanish heritage, middle-aged yet still slim and dark of hair, opened the door.

"May I please see Mr. Mellon?" Jessie asked. "My name is Jessica Starbuck, and I understand I'm expected."

"Of course! Welcome, Miss Starbuck, I'm Mrs. Mellon, and you're certainly honoring us by coming all this distance." As she ushered Jessie inside, Mrs. Mellon happened to glimpse Tino moving away from them. "Poor man's still ailing," she murmured.

"Is he sick, or injured? I didn't know."

"Wounded pride, a chronic male affliction, and not to be taken too awfully serious. He's a good man. Tino's been with us ten years, knows farming, and knows how to handle

47

men. Most of the time, that is." There was a winning smile on Mrs. Mellon's lips and a twinkle to her eyes. Jessie could not help liking her. "I do hope you can do something about our afflictions, Miss Starbuck. Gunther's having a meeting with some of the other farmers hereabout, and I'm afraid we're all at the end of our tether. Please, won't you sit down while I fetch him?"

"Thank you." Jessie settled on a couch and glanced around the spacious front parlor, as Mrs. Mellon crossed and went through an inner door. The furniture was of the sturdy variety, the main piece being a table at least fifteen feet long in the middle of the room. Under the table was a half-dozing sheepdog, who regarded Jessie with heavy-lidded brown eyes. It lay on an enormous Indian blanket that was serving as a rug, and other blankets, equally large, hung from the walls like tapestries.

Within three minutes Gunther Mellon strode into the room. "Miss Starbuck, I'm real glad you're here." Impetuously he stuck out his hand and shook Jessie's as though he were pumping water.

"I trust I can be of service," Jessie said, salvaging her hand. "I and Ki. Do I understand rightly that Ki went to Estero?"

"Yep, with one of m'boys. Seems to me he said he wanted to ask around about the *Paiute*, which got raided and torched last night. I expect them both back soon. Follow me."

Gunther Mellon escorted Jessie to the inner door, his stride long and rushed. He was a gray-headed man of strong will and stronger passions, and these had carved their lines in his tanned, serious face. He was a fraction under six feet, but his large frame was "gaunted down" so that his clothes hung on him loosely. A small, iron-gray moustache gave his features a rather stern look, but Jessie judged it wasn't sternness, but concern, which compelled him.

48

She too was concerned. "The *Paiute!* You mean it was—"

"Yes, yes, and believe you me, Miss Starbuck, your company had better start guaranteeing safe delivery, or we'll be as sunk as your boats. Not that shipping is our only problem—ah, that it were!—but it's still a major factor. Wheat has jumped in price again and should go even higher by the time we market our crop."

Jessie, following him quickly along a corridor, realized Mellon was in no more a mood to discuss Ki, or the *Paiute,* than his foreman had been. But Ki was safe, that was the important thing, and figuring that Ki would fill in the details when he returned, she switched to the topic obsessing Mellon. "What do you think the wheat will be worth?"

"I can't say to the dollar, but we should each make several thousand dollars. Enough to buy new land, horses and mules, seed and machinery, livestock—and with plenty left to pay our creditor."

"Fenton Chadwick?"

"How'd you know?"

"A lucky hunch" Jessie replied wryly.

Mellon went on to explain that six years before, during a terrible drought, he himself had borrowed four thousand dollars. He had recently paid the final installment to Chadwick, who had purchased the debt, but Chadwick had refused to return his note. "He claims it was for forty thousand, not four, and he has a stake in my ranch now!"

"No wonder he won't give you the note."

"That note, Miss Starbuck, shows one more zero that I ever recollect signing for," Mellon growled. "I think that damned—pardon me—Chadwick forged it. If he did, he did it real well. I've seen it, and to be honest, I can't tell it's been done."

Jessie followed him into a large patio, where there were

a couple of trees and an abundance of flowers. There was also a number of men standing or sitting about, some of Mellon's neighboring farmers whose homes were spread across this area of the valley. Mellon introduced Jessie, and she was impressed by their sturdy and proud demeanor, just as she was saddened by their impoverished look and, in the case of one man, a bandaged arm.

"I'll pay them killers back," the man vowed angrily.

Jessie shook her head. "But there must be law here!"

"Yeah, Sheriff Lester Dexter, and he's an old fool," the man answered. "I went to see him, but Chadwick got there first."

"Y'see, Chadwick had a dozen witnesses saying Frank here had drawn on him," Mellon explained, "when he an' his boys had gone a-callin' on Frank to collect a debt. I'm not the only one, Miss Starbuck, who's had to borrow money to keep going during the lean years. We've all signed notes and mortgages to get a little cash, and Chadwick's bought 'em up and, like I say, fiddled with 'em."

"He's an expert with a pen," another man declared.

"The sheriff's is a political job, too, and Chadwick has power here," a third added. "He's even a deputy sheriff!"

"Chadwick's brought in a bunch of toughs, men who have been disappointed hunting gold and're desperate. He feeds and liquors 'em and gives 'em a dollar now'n then, and they serve him. He's marshalling 'em like an army at the Odell ranch, after he dispossessed Odell and his family. It's the biggest place around," Mellon added, "and too close for comfort, too."

"Are they responsible for the raids and burnings?" Jessie asked. "I've heard you're having a rash of them as well."

"If you ask us," the second man responded, "it's the work of either Chadwick's crew or them river pirates on a fling. If you ask others, it's a bunch of owlhoots, including

50

one of Gunther's hands, Roger Page. Page has vanished and can't be located."

"Nobody knowing Page can believe he turned traitor, arranged fires, and skipped with the raiders," the wounded men stated. "Besides, he was engaged to your daughter, wasn't he, Gunther?"

Mellon sighed. "Not officially, but lots of jabber along those lines. I always thought he was a fine young man. Marryin' Honora would've fixed him up pretty nice for the future. I can't think he'd toss all that away for a share of what the raiders are gettin'."

"It doesn't seem reasonable," Jessie allowed. "Still, the lure of quick riches has turned many older and wiser heads."

"Riches! How d'you steal a field of wheat, or a barn full of farm machinery? You can't! The raiders are reaping nothing, but they're leaving us with nothing. It doesn't make any sense," Mellon said.

"There's always the chance, then, that Page is dead," Jessie added.

"It's been six weeks now, and nary a trace of the body. Or of the raiders. We've tried to track 'em, but keep losin' the trail out on those dusty roads, or when they wade in irrigation ditches," Mellon said.

The third man agreed, adding, "There's a lot of ground to cover, Miss Starbuck. It was my idea to start posting sentries, particularly at night, but whatever gang it is still manages to sneak through undetected. Besides setting our crops and buildings ablaze, there've been some clashes and a couple of drygulchings."

"Well, that'd indicate there might be a spy somewhere," Jessie said. "Can you trust all your men?"

"Probably not, especially this time of year when we hire so many itinerant workers for harvest. But it's our fight and we'll handle it. Your fight is out there on the river. It won't

51

do us much good to clean up our back yard if you can't move our cargo to—Honora!"

Mellon gaped blurting, as the patio wall gate burst open and a girl dashed in. She was in the first bloom of womanhood, petite and exquisite, with long dark hair and round flashing eyes—eyes, Jessie perceived, that were young versions of Mrs. Mellon's eyes. She was pale and distraught, yet there was a high tilt to her chin, which bespoke the pride of her high-bred maternal ancestry.

"Papa!" she cried. "Papa, I was in the barn when—"

Mellon harumphed. "Honora, mind your manners!"

His daughter flushed and curtsied to the guests, but was so wrought that she kept on talking in a torrent. "Juan just rode in from town, all in a lather! Papa, listen to me; Juan says that Ki has been arrested! Ki is an escaped convict, a fugitive wanted for murder!"

★

Chapter 5

The previous night, while Jessie had been romping in bed with Brockett, Ki had arrived in Estero with the other survivors of the *Paiute* thoroughly foot-worn, exhausted, and madder'n hell.

Estero crouched in a shallow bend of the San Joaquin River and displayed all the earmarks of being a lusty and tough end-of-river town. It was dominated by two structures, indicating its main livelihoods. The first, located on a central plaza, was a long, false-fronted building that combined the Feednseed General Store and the Roundheeler Pleasure Palace, the store taking up two-thirds of the space, along with a smaller barn in back. The second was the Indianhead warehouse and wharf, which was jammed with stacked bales, crates, and barrels, its broad dockyard carved and rutted by the iron tires of freight wagons carrying cargo to and from the fertile valley's interior.

At this late hour, though, the town was as dead as a tomb. The surrounding clusters of shops and houses were all dark and soundless, their streets empty and still, and even the palatial Roundheeler saloon was shuttered closed. The loudest things Ki found were the signs proclaiming Fenton Chadwick for Commissioner, which covered the town walls, and Indianhead's dockmaster when he was awakened at the warehouse and told of the disaster.

To his credit the dockmaster quickly took charge. He had the owner of the town's hotel rousted, so rooms and meals could be supplied at company expense, and tried to have the sheriff and the telegraph operator found, but to no avail. It was rumored, he confessed, that the sheriff and telegrapher were in a poker grudge match and had purposely gone someplace where they wouldn't be disturbed. He also promised to look into all claims of losses in the morning when his clerks would be there to help.

Not surprisingly the dockmaster had very little time for Ki. Nor did Ki expect preferential treatment. So, feeling that the situation was in capable hands and that there was nothing he personally could do till daylight, he went to the hotel and slept.

Rising just after dawn, Ki ate breakfast at the hotel and returned to the wharf. The dockmaster, who hadn't rested a wink, was already being bombarded by haranguing passengers, as well as by customers who'd come to pick up their freight from the *Paiute*. He was frazzled and curt with Ki, yet reluctantly agreed to lend Ki one of his saddle horses with gear.

The horse, which was stabled in an adjacent livery, was a deep-brisketed bay gelding of feisty temperament. It tried to nip Ki while being saddled and didn't settle in to being ridden until Ki had taken it galloping around the dockyard a few times in a rambunctious contest of wills. It matched, Ki thought, the dockmaster's personality, and he wondered if all the man's mounts were as unruly.

He walked the spirited bay to the plaza, where the telegraph office, along with the post office, was housed in one corner of the general store. Already the town was becoming crowded, buckboards and wagons almost as prevalent as horses, as shoppers pressed to run their errands before the searing midday heat—sure signs that come the cooler temperatures of evening, a lot of merry hurrawing would break loose from the saloons and gaming parlors.

The Roundheeler was open, but it was a tad early for

serious drinking, and the noises filtering from it were low and desultory. Ki was able to find an empty spot at the rack near its entrance, and tying the bay there, he walked along the building to the store.

Inside, Ki located the telegrapher, who slouched at his desk in a cubicle, looking as though he were suffering from a ferocious hangover. Concisely and in code, Ki wrote a message to Jessica about the *Paiute*, the dockmaster's competency, and his own plans to go on to Mellon's ranch, and addressed it in care of her hotel in Sacramento, unaware that Jessie was already riding on her way.

Paying, Ki asked: "You like cards?"

"I hate cards, poker in particular," the man groaned.

Well, if nothing else, Ki mused as he walked away, he'd learned who'd won the grudge match last night. He was opening the front door of the store, when he heard his bay gelding's distinctive high whinny and a man's harsh voice: "Hold the devil, Trent, while I—" The voice choked off.

Ki slammed the door and came out fast, catching a swift look at the setup. Ugly and stout, with a shaved, malformed head, a man in range clothes was scrambling under the rack, trying to dodge the rearing horse, his face ashen, his hat lying in the dust. Another man, taller and heavier and with a fat tomato of a nose, was attempting to grab the horse's bit without, in turn, being bitten.

The bald man didn't see Ki sprinting toward him. He was palming a revolver, murder in his eyes. "I'll learn that wild—"

Ki reached out and yanked him off balance. The man gave a wild yelp and tried to bring his revolver up. Ki knocked it out of his hand and jammed the heel of his right hand into the man's face. The man caromed against the cross pole of the rack so hard that he splintered it. He dropped, momentarily stunned breathless.

The man trying to grab the reins jerked for his pistol.

He only drew part-way, as Ki, springing the short distance with a leaping kick, caught him in the solar plexus. Ki purposely tempered his strike so that it would leave the man alive and merely wishing he were dead, but it was powerful enough to send the man careening back to slam the front walls of the saloon, his pistol flying.

The bald man was dragging himself away, turning a stricken face to the horse, which was rearing over him. Ki's soothing voice calmed the gelding to where it merely pawed and snorted testily. The second man, gasping for air, stumbled forward with one hand clutching his belly and his other fumbling for his pistol.

Ki punted the pistol aside. "Next time you want to fool around with any horse, make sure you get permission."

The second man, the one called Trent, grimaced and wheezed, "Hell, Damrow only wanted a look at him."

"Damrow must be near-sighted."

Damrow was rising to his feet—and he rose swinging. He'd crawled feebly to where he was almost behind Ki, acting as though the fight was out of him, and then lashed out to catch Ki unaware. He very nearly succeeded, but for Ki's glimpsing his move at the last instant.

A roundhousing haymaker crunched, grazing against Ki's jaw before he could fully swerve aside. The blow's meaty impact sent him staggering. Wincing with pain, Ki shook his head to clear it, falling back to regain his footing, his left heel accidentally stomping Trent's gun-wrist, Trent having used Damrow's sneak attack to try again for his pistol. Trent reeled, and along with his howls Ki could also hear sounds of men gathering, coming mostly from the saloon. The noises were confused, his head still ringing, but Ki didn't pay them any attention anyway, dismissing all vagrant subjects from his consciousness to focus on Damrow.

"Stand clear, boys, give him room to fall!" Damrow

called, contemptuous with confidence. "He's big for a Chink and'll hit hard!"

"He ain't fallin', Damrow, and he ain't gonna fall," Ki heard one of the spectators say.

"He's gonna hit the dirt," Damrow growled savagely. "Any of you gents know I only has to tap once to put an hombre's lights out."

It was then that Ki struck back with a jolting uppercut. As well-versed in unarmed combat as Ki was, he could have easily killed Damrow, killed him and Trent both with lightning speed, and a part of him was angry enough to do so. Yet it would've been an overreaction, too strong a punishment for the crime, and a breaking of his "doctrine of duress," *nkiomo-kammi,* which he'd sworn to when learning his martial arts. Moreover, he intuitively perceived that using methods that would seem strange and exotic would draw too much attention and might later backfire against him and this mission. Anyway, the rage and frustration pent up in him since the *Paiute* raid were rising to a boil, and he couldn't think of a better venting than to beat Damrow at his own game, the cruder yet accepted technique of the common brawl.

Ki followed the uppercut with a one-two combination. His punch started from his shoulder, went slightly upward, then smashed down like a club. Damrow tried to jerk his head backward to save himself, and he did, perhaps, save himself a broken skull. As it was, Ki's fist slashed down across his forehead, nose and chin, turning his face instantly into a blob of red and driving Damrow almost to his knees.

While he was in that squatting position, Ki's left fist hammered into his chest and hurled him, squawling, back into the circle of onlookers, where he lay still.

Now Ki turned slightly as, with a yell, Trent dived at him, and some of the bystanders joined in. A backward swing of Ki's arm caught Trent in the throat, flipping him

57

ass over bootheels into a saloon window, which shattered in a cascade of glass shards. Trent jackknifed inside, groaning feebly.

Another man made a wild grab for Ki. Pivoting aside, Ki snagged him by his belt and neck and heaved him down alongside the building toward the store. The man's body hit a display table of hair tonic and tumbled to the ground, the tonic bottles and table following. Then a chair whizzed past Ki's head, struck a support post of the overhang roof, and cracked it. The chair was one of a set used by loungers outside the saloon, but another chair came through the broken window a split-second later. Ki caught and tossed it right back at its sender, the chair nearly taking the fellow's head off.

By now the plaza was in a state of seige. Faces pressed to window panes, while other men and women hastened from doorways of nearby shops, shouting questions, answers, while converging on the fight. Ki swiveled to take on his next opponent, bitterness clouding his slate eyes as he flicked a disdainful glance at the ragged group forming deeper around him. They could've stopped it if they'd wished to, if they'd had the courage to step in.

He ducked a straight-arm knuckle-duster, one of his own fists connecting with another fighter's face, dropping the man like a sack of potatoes. Yet another man leaped on his back, encircling his throat with one arm and trying for a stranglehold. That arm was taken in a grip of iron, pulled straight out. Bending slightly, Ki hurled him through the air against two more attackers, the two collapsing, legs unhinged, and falling heavily on a senseless body.

The last of those siding with Damrow and Trent, a man whose face was not contorted in fear, tried to duck past Ki and head for the saloon's batwing doors. But Ki's hand speared out and took him by the neck while his other hand snared the slack of his pants. Lifting him, Ki gave him a twirl and sent him sailing through the doorway, just as one of the batwings opened and a bartender with a table-leg truncheon was about to step out. The man's body hit the bartender solidly and sent him tumbling back inside with a grunt of gasping breath. The doors swung shut, masking from view the scene of the resounding crash.

"Gawd, he downed Damrow right smart. An' Trent, he's still seein' stars," Ki heard somebody declare in awe.

Another gawker guffawed, "He tuckered the cream o' Chadwick's crew. By Christ, Lennie will stink of that hair oil for the next month!"

Without comment Ki brushed himself off and moved toward his horse, figuring he'd best get while the getting was good. Then a tall figure, clothing flapping on his bony form, thrust toward him, morning sunlight reflecting off the five-pointed badge pinned to the sweated flannel shirt.

"Hold it, you!"

Ki paused, sizing up the lawman. Long legs were encased in stained black pants tucked in high boots, and a battered felt hat was canted on his head, a few stray greasy locks showing, matted to his brow. A walnut-handled Colt rode at his skinny hip, and the badge he wore carried the words: Sheriff, Merced County. His long horselike face sported a thin, twitchy nose, eyes as greasy as his hair, and an expression of indignant outrage.

There was no sign of anger on Ki's face, except for the fact that one eye was squinting and his lips were drawn partly back from clenched teeth. He met the lawman's burning gaze and asked calmly, "Something bothering you, Sheriff?"

"Damn tootin' there is—you! What's your name?"

"Ki."

"That a first name or a last?"

"Both, together."

Somewhat disconcerted by this, the sheriff ran his eyes

59

up and down Ki's form. "Okay, uh, Ki, you just ridin' through?"

"Maybe. Does it matter?"

"It sure does." The sheriff gestured at the half-torn clothes and the blood streaking Ki's face and then at the sprawl of downed men who were in various stages of moaning and crawling. "It does, it sure does, when you pick Estero to do your feudin' in."

Ki shrugged. "What little I may've done was in self-defense. I'm carrying no quarrel with anyone here." Which was true enough, now. He leaned forward and whispered conspiratorially, "Tell you factually, from what I could tell of it, everyone slipped. Maybe they'd all been in the bar and had a snort too many."

"Listen, you," the sheriff said, setting his jaw, "I've got enough trouble, see, enough of it, without you making wise with more."

"You ask Damrow. You just ask him if he didn't slip."

The sheriff's thin brows lifted. He muttered, "We'll see," and he swept the gathered crowd with his gaze. "Some of you must've seen the beginning of the fight. Who started it? I'll jug him!"

Nobody answered. Men began to shift their feet nervously, glancing at one another, at Ki, and at the Chadwick crewmen. The sheriff grumbled under his breath, "I never seen it, not any of it myself. I was in my office and heard the ruckus."

"I slipped, Lester, like he says."

The unexpected admission surprised everyone, including Ki, for it came from Damrow. Ki turned, frowning, and saw a bystander gripping the woozy man by the elbow, helping him to his feet.

A man hidden in the back of the crowd gave out a loud, sardonic laugh. "He licked you square, barroom style."

"I slipped, we all slipped, and don't any of you forget it!"

The sheriff nodded grumpily. "Well, if you say so, Damrow, then that's that." Then jerking a thumb at the crewmen, he brusquely ordered, "Some of you rubberneckers take a hand with these guys."

The sheriff, plainly enough, took orders from Damrow, which meant he was under the thumb of Damrow's boss, the politico running for Commissioner, Fenton Chadwick. He stood for a moment, legs akimbo and hands on his hips, watching a few of the crowd go to first one and then another of the crewmen and hustle them back into the saloon. The rest of the crowd started to thin before they could be dragooned into helping. Ki made a motion as if to leave, but the sheriff turned to him, putting out an arm to stop him.

"Mister, just see to it you act like a gent in my bailiwick."

"I always obey the law of the land, Sheriff," Ki replied blandly. Keeping casual, he moved past his horse, unhitched it and swung up into saddle. As a languid gait, he rode toward the end of the plaza where, the hotel clerk had vouched, began the trail that led to Gunther Mellon's ranch.

Just before the edge of the plaza, Ki felt the impulse to shift about and glance back. The sheriff was striding away, and nobody else was paying him any mind. Nobody except Damrow, that is, who stood wiping blood from his face with a bandanna, staring after Ki. Staring with a look fit to kill.

Chapter 6

Ki followed the trail eastward through amber expanses of wheat. It was still early morning, and the heat was nowhere as intense as it soon would be, but he could feel the sweat stinging his scrapes and scratches on his chest and down his back.

About six miles from Estero the trail veered to parallel one of the numerous creeks which irrigated the valley and fed the San Joaquin River. He continued along the creek, and the rush of water, swifter here than it was close to town, reached him through the intervening screen of brush and trees. The sound suggested coolness, and unable to resist, Ki swung his horse in by the creek's edge to a small clearing shaded by cottonwood and cedar. White-laced water spilled over a small natural dam, forming a clear, shallow, very inviting pool.

His eyes lightened. As the bay stepped cautiously to nuzzle the water for a drink, Ki began stripping to the buff for a quick dip, eager to soak his bruises and cleanse himself and his clothes of the brawl's grime and blood. He dropped his vest and shirt on the bank and was just finishing removing his pants when a bullet cut leaves low over his head.

The bullet came from behind him, and he moved instinctively. Naked, he went over the bank in a shallow dive as the report of the bullet's firearm—a rifle, by its sound—cracked the stillness. The water was shockingly cold against his bare flesh. He kept submerged until he hit the current in the middle of the pool, then drifted with the flow. He recalled seeing that the pool's outlet was between two huge rocks, and when they loomed up, he surfaced slowly, took a deep breath, and let his body get carried between the rocks. The creek shallowed beyond, the water tumbling over rocks and small sand spills.

With the big rocks as cover, Ki stood up. The water reached his waist. Lowering himself, he pushed silently to the bank, where he heard voices. The first one was that of a woman, an older woman, to judge by its timbre. She spoke in Spanish, and her voice sounded frightened. A younger woman's voice answered, sharp and determined.

A few moments later a girl appeared on the bank where Ki had plunged into the pool. She was small and shapely with a lustrous dark sheen to her hair and eyes. Dressed in tan riding breeches, silk blouse, and a big sombrero, she was clutching a Winchester rifle and was peering into the pool as if seeking a target.

Frowning, Ki noiselessly eased out from behind the rocks and climbed on the bank. Padding closer, he overheard the girl tell the older woman standing behind her to hush so she could listen.

"Listen for what?" Ki asked, coming up behind them.

The girl whirled. The older woman threw up her hands and cried, *"Madre de Dios!"* Then she sank to her knees, squeezing her eyes closed and burying her face in the folds of her long black dress.

The girl, unnerved but resolute, brazenly stared at Ki as she whipped the rifle around and pointed it squarely at his navel.

Ki grinned and raised his hands. "Watch out," he said. "You might hit something you'll later regret having shot."

"I might," she agreed crossly, "but it'd be small loss."

63

"You've got eyes like ebony," Ki noted affably. "And there are three small freckles on the tip of your nose, and now you're blushing."

The girl stamped her foot. "Shut up! How dare you parade—"

"Why, I also see the two middle buttons are missing off your shirt," Ki interjected, grinning even wider. "Speaking of parading, I've never seen that part of a lady showing before."

The girl glanced down at herself hastily. With a long forward leap, Ki grabbed the rifle from her hand. She glared at him wildly, her dark eyes furious. Ki just kept on grinning.

"And that's a trick that would never work with a man, miss. I just naturally don't let people, even pretty girls, shoot at me."

For a moment she tried to wrestle him for the rifle, then suddenly let go and reached down in her boot. Ki flung the rifle down as he saw her hand rise with a slim-bladed knife. To hell with this, he thought grimly, catching her wrist and spinning her around.

"Let go of me, you, you brute!"

"All right," Ki said amiably and shoved.

The girl, arms windmilling, made an ungraceful bellyflop into the pool. Her geysering splash showered Ki, but he stayed at the edge of the bank until she surfaced. She floundered at first, then began treading water, her dark hair loose around her face, her black eyes sizzling with sparks.

Seeing she wasn't in danger of drowning, Ki slowly, unconcernedly pulled on his clothes. The girl remained in the water, absolutely livid. The fat Mexican woman raised her eyes to Ki when he was mostly dressed, then lowered them again and began praying. Ignoring her chanting wails, Ki picked up the rifle, removed the shells, and tossed the

64

weapon over the girl's head into the pool.

"Here's another lesson," he called to her. "Some diving practice, if you want it. Might cool you off some, too." His good humor returned as he shrugged into his vest. "Besides, that was no way to welcome a stranger, miss."

Her lips curled. "No Chadwick rider is welcome!" she retorted, sputtering water.

Ki shook his head. "I don't work for Chadwick."

"Then who are you?"

"You should've asked that before." Smiling, he turned to the prayerful woman, and when she looked up, frightened, he patted her shawled head. Then he climbed aboard the bay, gave the girl a final mocking salute, and rode out of the shady clearing.

As Ki jogged on, he was still grinning. The girl, in spite of her short size and gamin beauty, had spunk, a recklessness of spirit, and a cool daring. Her pixiness also hid the fact she was no longer a little girl. She was about twenty, Ki judged, certainly no younger than eighteen, which made her a woman. And by the gleam in her eyes when she surveyed his nude body, Ki had a hunch she was already a woman who knew what to do with a man.

Soon the creek turned southerly, and the trail continued east, dipping up and down with high grain again flanking both sides. Ki tried to keep sharp lookout for any more gun-wielding surprises, yet keen-sighted as he was, he couldn't penetrate very far past the fence rows, especially with the rising sun ahead glaring pointedly in his face.

About late morning he came upon the entrance drive to some big rancho, as Californian landowners were prone to call their spreads. This one was evidently so vast that he couldn't even perceive the end of its drive, much less any main house or grounds. Nor did it appear very friendly, the shoulders of the entrance sprouting *NO TRESPASS* and

65

KEEP OUT signs, and the drive itself barred by a padlocked wrought iron gate.

Nonetheless he reined in, thinking perhaps this might be Gunther Mellon's farm. He searched for some indication of the owner's name and found that the freshly painted warning on one sign covered some other letters underneath. Scrutinizing closely, he could make out the words: *J. J. ODELL, PROP.* Whoever J. J. Odell was, or had been, this was obviously not Mellon's property, so Ki jigged his horse onward.

Soon he rode by a couple of narrow lanes. These cut off to the south, whereas the drive had sliced north; yet they too were barred, this time by long plankboards haphazardly nailed across the gaps in the fencing, as though these had been erected as barricades instead of gates. Except for that, the lanes resembled the sort of seldom-used paths that traversed the back acreages of farms.

Something he couldn't quite fathom began to warn Ki as he moved on. His feeling of tenseness, of something about to happen, kept growing like a persistent itch. Finally when he reached a third boarded-up lane, Ki reined in again to see if he could scratch some reason out of his nagging discomfort.

It was his horse that caught on first. Suddenly the bay sniffed and thrust its head as if bird-dogging toward the wheat.

"Halt and hike!" a peremptory challenge rang out.

It came from the wheat. Ki still couldn't see into its thickness, and he doubted his horse could either, but he knew that men must be lying where the bay was staring, just beyond the fence on the near side of the lane.

"I'm already stopped," he replied, raising his hands. "Hold your fire, whoever you are. I'm just looking for Gunther Mellon's place."

66

"Oh yeah? What d'you want with Mellon?"

"That's between me and him. He's expecting me."

He kept his hands shoulder-high to show good faith and hoped his ambushers were partial to Mellon, not against him. Now he glimpsed faint movements in the wheat and heard murmurings of a low-voiced conference. Presently a tow-headed young man in bib overalls emerged from the field, an old Remington revolver held level in his grip as he warily approached Ki.

"You're covered by more'n him," the man who'd spoken before called from his hiding place. "My son Tim'll take good care of your weapons and'll hand 'em back soon's we fetch you to Gunther."

"I'm not packing," Ki said and slowly, gingerly, he opened his vest to show he wasn't carrying any firearms.

The young man circled the horse, studying it and Ki. Although alert, he was searching for telltale bulges of concealed handguns and was blind to the thin daggers and seemingly flat pockets of *shuriken* which lined Ki's vest. Nor did he spot the curved knife behind Ki's waistband, or consider the lead-weighted rope belt as anything more than a cheap substitute for real leather.

Satisfied, he called back, "He's clean, Dad."

A brawny, light-haired man now straightened in the wheat and waded toward them. The family resemblance was striking, and he also was wearing overalls, as were the three other men who rose trailing him, rifles in the crooks of their elbows.

"Cap'n Inglenook, at your service," the man said, as they grouped around Ki. "We're a mite touchy here, as you can see. We're starting our harvest, and things have been happening."

Ki introduced himself and replied that he understood.

"Gunther's down the section a piece. We'll break open

67

the lane and you go on slow, and I'll follow. My horse is hid in the next dip. Tim, you and the boys stick tight and guard."

Fifteen minutes later, Ki and Captain Inglenook were moving through the field and crossed over a low rise. There Inglenook retrieved his ground-reined pinto and mounted, and adhering to the military method of riding slightly behind and to the left of Ki, he escorted him deeper into the wheat. The ripe grain flowed on and on across the gently rolling terrain, unruffled by wind, a golden ocean with the aspect of waves arrested in motion.

Eventually they reached a hillock from which they saw horse-drawn reapers cutting wide swaths in the wheat. "There's Gunther over yonder, bossin' the job," Inglenook said. "Let's high-step it."

They kicked their horses into a fast trot, Inglenook still carefully keeping his position as they forged a path through the field. When they were near enough to be heard, Inglenook stood in his stirrups and waved to Mellon, calling out in a stentorian voice, "Gunther! Here's the man you wanted to see!"

The rugged, gray-thatched farmer turned to survey Ki while they approached and reined in, his eyes quizzical and utterly devoid of recognition. Inglenook scowled leerily at Ki.

"Thought you told me Gunther's expecting you."

"He is; he just doesn't know it yet," Ki replied pleasantly and, facing Mellon, introduced himself. "Miss Starbuck was delayed in Sacramento," he explained quietly, "but will be on her way today or tomorrow. I came on ahead in hopes of getting a jump on—"

"Starbuck! Burn me afire, I've been fretting you'd never arrive." Mellon thrust up his hand to shake. "It's good to meet you, Ki. Me'n my friends are in a desperate plight. All we want is to be left alone so we can work and make a living, but it seems like fate stabs us every time we turn our back. If Starbuck can straighten even a little of it out, I'll be eternally beholden."

"Well, we'll do what we can," Ki answered noncommittally.

Inglenook, who'd been stewing with revived suspicions, blinked and scratched his head. "Didn't take long to get acquainted," he remarked. "But Gunther's the salt of the earth, and if he vouches for you, Ki, his say-so is plenty enough for me."

"It's plenty near noon, too," Mellon said, squinting at the sun. "Let me take you home for lunch, Ki, and I'll fill you in on our miseries. Dick, will you see to it the crew is fed?"

Inglenook readily agreed, and Mellon, wiping his face with a kerchief, hurried off to collect his horse. Minutes later he and Ki were riding toward his ranch house, a short run from the reaping.

Along the route Mellon talked in his clear if gruff manner, and Ki quickly gathered how the night attacks and burnings, the suspect loans and local politics, were squeezing Mellon and his friends to ruin. The river raids were also damaging, but on the surface they were a separate problem, Indianhead's problem, which indirectly hurt the farmers. Yet by the time the house loomed into view, Ki was wondering if there might be more of a connection, the raids somehow linked to the crippling combination of menaces here.

At the moment, though, all appeared serene and untrammeled. Ascending the broad knoll that was shaded by great trees, Ki gazed admiringly at Mellon's spacious home, a don's hacienda, with all the necessary barns, stables, outbuildings, and corrals. When at last they entered the broad main yard, Ki saw it was bustling with activity. Men too old and boys too young for field labor, and women ranging from lass to grandmother, were all working earnestly at their appointed tasks, while from the kitchen filtered tantalizing odors of cooking.

Ki surveyed the men in passing, just as he had the crew back at the reaping. A good bunch, he decided. But none of them looked like a gunman, and it was gunmen Mellon and his friends would probably need to protect their farms. They were just that, farmers and farmhands, nothing more. They might be able to aim and fire, all right, but with the possible exception of Captain Inglenook, they wouldn't know any tricks of the fighting trade.

As he and Mellon drew up to the hitchrail fronting the porch, some of the nearby workers paused or moved closer, greeting Mellon with waves and cheery hellos. Only one man came all the way over, a somber, middlin'-sized fellow in shirt, jeans, and straw hat, his eyes, hair, and skin color suggesting a deep Hispanic bloodline.

"Mr. Mellon, the rakes on thrasher four broke, and—"

"What, again? Well, let it go till after lunch." Mellon turned to Ki. "This's Tino Benedict, my foreman. Tino, meet Ki. He's here to root out some of our troubles, him and a Miss Starbuck, who's comin' soon. I want you to help them all you can and give them the same trust you do me—or yourself."

The foreman reared perplexed. "You brought them to—"

"Yep, at my special invitation."

For a moment Tino seemed to struggle with his tongue. Then coldly he said, "No disrespect intended, Mr. Mellon, but what the devil's got into you? Why, they're total strangers!"

"Not entirely, but I'm willing to take whatever risk there is. If I'm wrong, nothing's lost, 'cause we're licked the way we're going."

Tino shifted to confront Ki. Matching his skeptical stare,

70

Ki sensed the foreman to be honest, loyal, and implacably distrustful. What's more, he was a fighter, belligerent by nature and with a temper that might be explosive if unchecked.

Whatever Tino was gearing to say was never said, for the lengthy silence was broken by sounds of a buggy wheeling into the yard. Tino's stern face softened, and Mellon began grinning.

"Brace yourself, Ki," Mellon said, good-humored with pride. "You're about to have the pleasure of meeting my daughter, Honora."

The buggy pulled up in the middle of the yard and a girl jumped down from the seat, turning the one-horse rig over to the hostler who came to meet her. An older woman climbed down primly after her.

Ki settled back on his feet, a faint smile crinkling the corners of his eyes. The girl coming toward them, walking with quick, free stride, was the girl he'd dumped in the creek.

Honora Mellon still smoldered. Her clothing was still damp from her dunking, but her anger was a live fire that flared brightly as she recognized Ki standing beside her father. Her stride faltered and she stopped short to face them, pertly curvacious, her breasts pushing against the damp sheen of her silk blouse, her lips slightly parted, baring a hint of white teeth.

"Honora this's Ki. Ki, this's my daughter and her *duenna,* Marie."

"We've met, Papa," Honora said frigidly. "Most unhappily."

Mellon looked puzzled. Tino looked concerned and more leery of Ki than ever. And Marie looked anguished, wringing her hands and moaning, "I warned her, Señor Mellon, but she would not listen."

71

"What warning? What happened?" Mellon demanded and turned on Ki. "What'd you do to her, to make Honora not like you?"

"I refused to be a gentleman and let her shoot me."

Mellon choked, Tino scowled, and Honora gradually began smiling. She was fire and violence, this girl, and proud as hell, but she also had graciousness and a sense of humor lacking in her father and the foreman. She tried stifling her smile, but it seeped out anyway, especially when Tino snarled pugnaciously at Ki, "You lie! You took unfair advantage of Honeydew—er, Honora!"

"He did not, Tino, stop it!" Honora said and appealed to her father. "I'm the one to be scolded. I mistook Ki for a Chadwick coyote, but I only shot to scare him, not kill him. Ki didn't scare; he tossed me in the creek instead." She smirked slightly. "Still, I dare say Ki will admit he thought he was, ah, barely escaping."

"Waaah!" Marie wailed and covered her face with her hands.

Mellon shook his head and Tino simmered down, muttering. Mellon sighed, "It's all too confusing. But no matter. You'd better go get changed, Honora, before your mother sees you."

Honora nodded and strolled past them, smiling at Ki. Marie followed her, averting her eyes from Ki as though she feared he'd jump out of his clothes at her. Mellon was still shaking his head.

And Tino erupted with all the hostility that had been building within him. "There! Y'see, Mr. Mellon? You didn't know about him and Honora, did you? What else is he keeping secret from us?"

"Who gives a damn!" Mellon snapped. "I don't. I'm just tickled pink somebody from outside finally is interested in helping us. Tino, please, if you have any loyalty toward me, show it now."

The foreman stood stiffly, clenching his big hands. "Mr. Mellon, I'd go to hell'n back for you. You know it, too. Well, this's near hell as I'll ever be alive, I reckon. I—I'll do like you ask." Then Tino eyed Ki. "But it don't mean I like it, or you."

That seemed to satisfy Mellon, if nobody else. "Okay, I'll see you after lunch about the thrasher, Tino. Ki, let's get you set in one of the guest rooms and then tie on the feed bag."

Ki nodded to Tino, who glowered sullenly back, and followed Mellon into the house. He felt, now, there was more to Tino's animosity than mere mistrust of outsiders, and that whatever it was, it was goading the foreman into branding Ki as the enemy.

Mellon was more interested in discussing his daughter. "Good thing Honora was smiling. Usually she takes a poke at anyone calling her Honeydew. She should've been a boy. Or maybe she's trying to make up for 'em," he continued, showing Ki into a room. "She had two brothers, y'see, but the older drowned in the Sacramento, and the younger was taken as a baby by fever."

"How tragic. I'm sorry to hear that."

"God's will. Wash up, and come to the dining hall."

The guest room was comfortably furnished and had windows and doors opening out onto the patio. Ki freshened himself, then found his way to the dining hall, which was dominated by a huge stone fireplace and a long, wide banquet table that groaned under the weight of all the food.

Mellon sat at the head of the table and his charming wife at the foot, where she kept urging Ki to have another helping of this dish or that. Honora was not present, and Ki was the only guest. During the meal nothing more was said about his and Jessie's mission, and Ki made a valiant effort to prove his appreciation of the cooking by eating fair to bursting.

73

They were digging into dessert when a maid rushed in. "Men here," she said fretfully. "The sheriff and that Chadwick!"

Chapter 7

Mellon sprang up, telling his wife, "Luisa, stay here."

Ki left his chair and followed Mellon out to the porch. In the yard, he saw five men just dismounting from their horses, one of them being the sheriff, his cheek bulging with tobacco cud. Another was a fancy-dressed dude, undoubtedly Fenton Chadwick. Their three companions were hardcases along the lines of Damrow and Trent, gun-heavy thugs who, like their boss, were being sided by the law— or what passed for it hereabouts.

Tino Benedict was also in the yard. He stood glaring at the visitors, standing midway between them and the porch but more to the left, one hand awkwardly clenching an old .36 Navy Colt. He was saying, "We got nothing to discuss with the likes o' you!"

And Chadwick retorted in the same instant, "I'm here to talk to the boss, not to his hired hands."

Ki, coming to a halt with Mellon at the edge of the porch, sized up Chadwick as being a squat, broad man with one of those homely, frank faces people instinctively take for honest. He had plain brown hair carefully combed and the assured voice of one who's in the right. Yet in that instant, Ki read other, subtler signs: the quick-sliding gray eyes behind spectacles that masked their penetrating quality; the flat-lipped mouth that hinted at ruthlessness; the manner of moving that indicated crafty forethought.

Ki also saw the foreman stepping back, saw the rage in

75

his direct eyes, and the pistol trembling in his angry grip. The sheriff, paling, stopped chewing. The other three men appeared to be casual observers, quite indifferent, yet Ki sensed that each of them was poised on trigger-tension, ready to react to the slightest warning. Tino, he knew, was treading dangerously.

"Ease up," Mellon said quietly to Tino, then looked past the foreman at Chadwick. "State your business, and make it snappy."

Chadwick advanced a pace, a loose smile playing over his lips. He gave Tino an almost sneering glance, eyed Ki with narrow-lidded interest, then regarded Mellon. "Very well, we'll talk right here, before everyone. You're two months in arrears, and I want the loan brought current, now, both payments plus late interest."

"Fat chance." Mellon said tightly. "I told you then, when you refused to return the note, that I'd repaid all four grand."

"The amount of this is forty thousand," Chadwick replied, holding up a legal document so Mellon could read the figures. "It also has a rider allowing me to call for the entire balance due after thirty days default. And I *will* call, if you don't pay up."

Mellon stiffened. "Either you or some other scoundrel has raised the figure on that note, Chadwick. Do your damndest!"

"As you wish. You may yet see fit to honor your debts, after I take you to court and win a quit-claim deed to your farm."

"You do, and you won't find us easy as the Odells and the rest you've cheated," Honora declared, suddenly appearing from the house to stand alongside her father. "You've burned our crops and shot at our crew, but you'll never force us off our property!"

Chadwick assumed an injured expression, but Ki could detect the irony behind it. "Why, Miss Mellon, you're letting your young imagination run away with you. I've suffered more from this outlaw gang than anyone else. In fact, only this morning six of my top hands were brutally assaulted by that man there beside you."

Honora gasped, but Mellon tensed purse-lipped. Ki, like Mellon seemed to, sensed the drift of Chadwick's remarks, and he wasn't surprised when Mellon responded in an ice-edged tone, "Are you charging Ki with purposely attacking your men?"

"There's still a mix o' opinions about that," the sheriff interjected sourly. "Nary a doubt, though, of Doc Hodges bein' up to his armpits with busted bones and cracked ribs, all caused by him. They're still pickin' glass slivers outta Trent, and Lennie locked hisself in the icehouse and won't come out 'cause he smells so bad. Pretty smart, your guy there. He's a fisticuff expert, not a gunsharp, and I can't even arrest him for disturbin' the peace without jugging the ones he whumped to a pulp, too."

"Uh-huh. And are you blaming me for having imported a pugilist for just that reason, to beat up on innocent folk?"

"Ain't prepared to say, Mellon, not till I've more proof."

Chadwick added, "Sheriff Dexter's only doing his duty. I can't imagine anyone thinking, however, that by siccing a bully on my men he'd intimidate me. Can you?"

Chadwick's question hung thick in the air, his tone and matter insinuating it was an accusation. Mellon and his daughter both quivered with indignation and throttled emotion. But Ki's attention was focused on Tino, whose blunt face was beginning to show danger signals again. Slowly Ki eased forward to reach a spot nearer the foreman, trying to gauge the temper boiling volcanic within him.

Ki was none too soon. Tino ripped out a sudden oath and made a wild upswing with his pistol. "Damn you! Mr. Mellon never—"

Ki dived, grasping the foreman's gunwrist in an *atemi*

hold that caused him to drop the pistol. At the same time, the sharp edge of Ki's left hand chopped hard, but not lethally, against the side of Tino's neck. Tino folded sprawling, glassy-eyed.

There was a faint, air-sucking gasp from Honora, and a startled grunt from her father, and outcries from some of the ranch hands who'd been gathering a safe distance away. Ignoring them, Ki pivoted to face Chadwick and his three sidekicks, who stood frozen in the yard with their revolvers half drawn. Sheriff Dexter was visibly shaken, looking as if he'd swallowed his chaw.

"Okay," Ki stated tersely. "The show's over."

Chadwick smiled again, softly. "You're pretty smart, all right."

"Smart enough to catch your trick, Chadwick. You'd like Tino to make a play, wouldn't you, so your gunnies would have an excuse to cut him down. And you brought along this spineless dupe of a lawman so he could back your action, however it turned out."

The sheriff turned red. "That's a lie! I'm upholdin' the forces of law'n order, and investigatin' mayhem and—"

"You're a tool in a crooked game, and you know it," Ki interrupted coldly. "If you're honest, you got the guts of a dead rabbit."

Mellon cleared his throat and spat derisively. "Ki's hit the nail on the head. Now clear out of here, all of you."

Chadwick smiled once more, mockingly. "We'll meet again." He remounted his horse and the others trailed him out of the yard.

When they were out of sight, Ki glanced around. Tino still lay unconscious. The ranch hands huddled, looking on with puzzled interest. Mellon had already stomped back inside the house, partly to calm his wife and partly to emphasize Ki's declaration that the show was over. Honora stood wan and nervous for a moment longer, then moved across to Ki and lightly touched his arm.

"I want to talk to you. Come in with me, please."

Ki stepped after her through the doorway and into the parlor, which was a cool and curtain-dimmed oasis from the increasingly hot day. There was sufficient light, though, for Ki to spot a slumbering dog under a big table . . . and for him to see the anguish etched on Honora's face, her eyes courageous, hoping without much hope.

"I–I have to thank you, Ki, for how you handled things out there. If it hadn't been for you, Tino would've been shot, maybe dead."

"He's a good man," Ki said gently, for in her anxiety he read that she understood the foreman better than most, and perhaps cared about him more than she realized. "Tino's loyal and unafraid, but that hot blood of his is apt to land him in a peck of trouble."

"And Chadwick's certainly the one to make trouble. He's a crook! I *know* he is. But he's got everyone bluffed or scared, even the law. He's forced out others around here till we're the only really big farm left, and now he's planning to dispossess us."

"Using that doctored loan as a club." Ki shrugged. "Well, let him try. My guess is it'd take him many months, maybe years, to push his claim through the courts, what with appeals and delays."

"You truly think so?"

"Sure, if you put up a fight."

"We can fight, and will. But none of us knows how to mount the kind of fight needed to be rid of Chadwick once and for all." Impetuously, Honora clutched Ki by the shoulders. "You do. It's plain to see. Chadwick saw it; that's why he tried trumping up those charges, to make you leave or get you arrested. He doesn't want anyone against him who's as hard and deadly as he is himself."

Her words bit into Ki, and he felt stung by her impression

79

of him—as though he were a machine, useful yet insensitive to pain and death. Strangely, at the same time he pitied Honora—pitied and desired to comfort her. She was desperate, despairing, but was plucky and determined to battle by any means fair or foul.

Ki wasn't sure, right then, if he more resented or respected the girl. He was sure she intrigued him. Then, without thinking, he responded to an impulse, and lifting her head, he kissed Honora tenderly, full on the lips.

Honora was limp and submissive in his embrace, and her mouth was warm against him. For a moment, just a moment, she returned his kiss. Then she broke away, startled, breathing hard. "I . . . I . . ."

Ki smiled lightly. "You want me to say I'm sorry?"

"You better be sorry, you skunk!" a voice snarled behind him. Ki wheeled to see Tino Benedict's muscular shape at the door, his .36 Colt pistol lifting, pointing. "You can't pull that!"

Ki started to leap forward. But Honora was closer, quicker, flinging herself between them. "No, Tino, don't you dare!"

Tino froze, his eyes blazing. "Stand aside, Honeydew. This *zoquete* don't fool me, and won't get away with maulin'—"

"Ki wasn't," she retorted, her voice abrubtly cool.

The pistol in Tino's hand drooped, and his face crimsoned. He stared at Honora as though disbelieving his ears, his expression changing from rage to bitterness and jealousy. Ki knew, then, what he'd suspicioned might lay behind the foreman's distrust and dislike of him: Tino was in love with Honora.

The thought stopped there. Tino almost yelled, "So that's how the wind blows, is it? And you're supposed to be almost engaged to Roger Page. Honeydew, you can't expect me to swallow a thing like this. You can't, and I won't. Hell—I quit!"

He heeled about and stalked out of the house. Honora made a lunge after him, her hand outstretched, but Ki stopped her.

"Hold tight, let me get him. Don't worry."

Tino was already halfway across the yard when Ki reached the porch. Sprinting, Ki almost caught up when Tino heard him and jerked around, eyes wild, trigger finger squeezing for a pointblank shot.

Ki was anticipating just such a move, after Tino's irrational actions in the house. Charging low, he blocked the rising gunarm, his shoulder ramming into ribs and his leg hooking behind an ankle. The foreman tripped backwards, sprawling flat in a cloud of dust . . . and he was toppling, Ki snatched the pistol and flung it away.

"Easy," he cautioned, waiting for Tino to get up.

Tino got up, but wasn't easy about it, rushing Ki with fists windmilling. Ki sidestepped and rabbit-punched Tino as he went past. Tino dropped, sliding on his face, rolled over, and came to his feet, his madness pitching him forward again. Ki's only impulse was to knock some sense into the man, so he met him with a stiff-fingered *yonhon-nukite* blow under the heart. Tino gasped breathless, tottered, then slumped over and down for good.

Bishop stepped back and glanced around. The ranch hands who'd chanced to be in the yard to see it, were again murmuring among themselves. Honora had seen it, too, from the porch where she stood, clasping a post with both hands. There was nothing Ki could tell any of them that'd do much good, so he strode to a trough by the corral and came back with a bucket of water.

Tino groaned when Ki doused his face. Ki hesitated a moment, then picked up the foreman's limp body and hauled him across to what appeared to be the main bunkhouse. The small bunch of men there pulled away from the steps, opening a path. Ki lowered Tino onto a bunk, then eyed the hands hovering about the doorway. "Out!"

They obeyed instantly, except for one old Mexican. Brown as cured leather, he grinned through his straggly gray beard, and when he spoke, he had the peculiar habit of referring to himself in the third person. "You looks to Juan like prime stock. Juan's seen few *japonés* but *muchos combatientes* in his day, and he never been wrong before. I don't think you'll break my string now."

Ki grinned. "I'll remember that, Juan."

The old man ducked out, cackling rustily, an Ki looked down at Tino. Consciousness was seeping back to the foreman now. He blinked and sat up, woozily holding his chest with both hands.

"Tino, that girl needs you now more than ever before, and so does her father. You're acting the fool, running out on them."

Tino stared, struggling to speak. He gave up; he was licked, showed he knew it, and was just a bit ashamed.

Or so Ki figured as he continued, "All I'm trying to do is help. But the Mellons need your help more than mine because you'll be here long after I'm gone—or anyway, you should be. All right, you saw something that shouldn't have been. It doesn't mean a damn, not one damn. It . . . Well, it just happened, is all."

Tino remained silent, eyes downcast. Ki left him alone then, feeling that if the rift weren't patched now, more words wouldn't heal it.

Outside, he saw Gunther Mellon striding toward him. Mellon looked intense but somewhat distracted, for Juan was keeping pace alongside, talking a blue streak and gesturing with relish.

When they met, Juan said, "I was relating how you—"

"Thanks," Ki said, and regarded Mellon. "I'm sorry."

"So am I, especially about the gun. I don't know or care

what provoked Tino; he deserved a pasting for such a crazy stunt."

"Well, it's over and done, and he's just fine."

"That's good. Y'know, long as I've known Tino, he's been rock steady, but after Page disappeared, he's acted strange, on the prod. Maybe you knocked the burrs off him, and I'd not be sorry for that."

Earlier, en route to his ranch, Mellon had told Ki of Page's vanishing. And Ki wasn't surprised by Tino's getting upset over it. But go berserk? Hell, Honora had more cause, grieving lovelorn, frantic from gossip of Page's deserting her and turning bad. Yet she was the steady one. An odd twist, which Ki filed away so he could focus on another aspect, one he'd been curious about for a while.

"I know you and the other farmers depend on Indianhead for all your bulk shipping," Ki said to Mellon. "What I don't know is if Chadwick uses Indianhead, and if not, who he does use. Maybe an outfit we haven't heard of, very small, trying to get a toehold."

"Nope, Indianhead's the only one. Still, I've never seen him or his freight at the dock, for whatever that's worth. Why?"

"Just curious. Sometimes companies play dirty tricks on rivals, or shippers make claims for ruined cargo that isn't, or doesn't exist."

"Ask me, Chadwick would stoop to any angle you can figure."

"Probably learn more in Estero," Ki pondered aloud. "Might nose around town this afternoon, unless you've need of me here."

"Nothin' that won't keep. Juan, get Ki's horse rigged."

"And Juan will go, too, on errands, *verdad?*"

Mellon gave his permission, and Juan took Ki to the stable. Fed and rested, the bay gelding was back to its old ornery self, so Juan gratefully let Ki do the saddling, while he got a sorrel ready for himself. They were just finishing when Honora strode in.

"There you are, Juan. Quick, west forty's crew needs you."

"Ah no, Señorita Mellon, Juan rides to town."

"Juan rides to repair broken harnesses," she retorted waspishly. "Or do you expect the teams to push the reapers?"

Juan sighed. "A long way for a long task," he lamented, but nodded acquiescence. "Amigo, Juan will catch up with you in town, fast as he can." And, as he led his sorrel rearward to the tack room, he called back: *Hasta luego! Save him a beer!*"

Ki began walking his gelding to the front, Honora stepping with him. She said, "I'll ride with you. I know a shortcut."

"Another time, Honora."

"You don't want me along?"

"I don't want you hurt." Ki paused outside the stable door. "I'm going to be looking around, to be down-dirty snooping. I'm not sure in where or for what, or how dangerous it might become."

"Well, you haven't seen the last of me," she vowed with a sly wink. When Ki mounted, she added, "I can be a pest," and stood waving as Ki rode across the yard toward the main drive.

The sun was scarcely past its zenith, a hot ingot high in the cloudless sky. It soon became a scalding weight against Ki, and by the time he reached the wagon road, his gelding's withers were already starting to froth and gleam. There were no trees, was no shade for a breather, so he moved on steadily, not pushing his horse.

Ki wasn't exactly thrilled at returning to Estero, but pre-

84

ferred to try stirring things up there to mucking about the ranch. He'd covered the farming peril pretty well for now, he felt, and wouldn't learn much more by sticking around ... idly waiting for Jessies, rubbing Tino's raw nerves, maybe prompting more hassle ... even, perchance, fiddling with Honora, if he were dumb enough to disregard her father and that half-loco foreman. He was dumb enough, Ki had to admit, recalling the fracas in the parlor. No, he and the ranch could do with a short break.

Shortly he passed the three boarded lanes, and then the iron-barred drive. The road was more familiar now, and he pressed along, willing to ride slowly but not to stop. Frequently he'd check his backtrail and sides, but saw nothing except the unraveling ribbon of road, and the heat-wavy gold image of stretching fields.

Pretty soon the creek joined in flanking, and not long after came the wide border strip of trees and brush. It looked refreshing, as inviting as before; and when he faintly heard rushing water from the other side of the greenery, Ki chuckled softly from the memory of what had happened earlier at that concealed little pool.

Then he heard "Ki..."

He jerked on the reins, abruptly alert, and swiftly peered around. Not a soul. Nor could he detect any slight movements, any telltale rustlings. The voice had been a low whisper, untraceably vague, yet clearly feminine and somehow sounding like Honora. That, of course, was absurd. Most likely the sound of an errant breeze, and he'd imagined the rest. His brain must've addled from too much sun, Ki thought disgustedly, and juggered his horse forward.

"Oh, Ki–i..."

This time it was louder and unmistakable. "Honeydew!" Ki stared at the woods, still not seeing her. "How'd you get here?"

"Shortcut, remember?" Her girlish laugh echoed from dense undergrowth. "C'mon, I've got something important to show you."

Ki angled off the road into the trees. Light footfalls were coming from ahead, but listening sharply, Ki detected they were moving farther away, not closer to him. "Little vixen," he muttered, dismounting and leading his horse as he went after her.

Honora's trail was easy to trace. Ki forged his own path across the matted copse, but didn't manage to intercept her until, plowing through some entangling foliage, he found himself out on the creekbank and very near the clearing overlooking the pool. Even then, he saw her horse before he saw the girl. A splotched pinto was tethered on the clearing's far side; it gave a low whinny, and Ki's gelding pawed a foreleg in response.

Exasperated, he called, "Okay, you're a pest," and headed toward the pinto. "What've you got to show that's so important?"

"Me!"

From the tall shrubbery behind her horse, Honora emerged into the bright sunlight. She was stark, bare-assed naked. And toeing delicately yet openly to mid-clearing, she seemed blithely unabashed, as if she savored Ki's startled attention.

Attention! Ki was all eyes, absorbed by her nude display. Her breasts, pertly jutting with ripe blackberry nipples; her flat belly, flaring into a rich froth of curls and the buried hint of fleshy lips; her boyish thighs, tapering into taut legs that he sensed could squeeze like nutcrackers when impassioned.

"I got to see what you have," she teased, as they moved toward each other. "Now you get to see what I have." And when they met, she pressed close with hands kneading his waist and began loosening his shirt from his pants, purring while she tugged, "Greedy me. I want to see what you have again."

What Ki had was a stiffening bone. Her game was arousing, but he wondered if it was quite so simple. She'd been mad this morning and coy this noon, and playing the wanton now could be to get at him as easily as it could be to get with him. He tried a roundabout stab to find out. "No complaints, Honeydew, but aren't you engaged to be engaged?"

"I hope I am. Roger's a catch, a very nice boy." Honora pouted, her hands freeing more shirt. "You're not a boy."

"I'm not nice, either."

"No, but I bet you're good."

Well, hell, Ki thought, and kissed her. She responded with enthusiasm, lips clinging hungrily, breasts mashing against his chest, small hands shifting to rub along his hips. They broke for air, but she continued to grip intimately, stretching on tiptoe.

"I wanted you, Ki; I wanted to right on the parlor rug."

"We got in enough mess. Anyway, a dog had the rug."

"Max would've moved. He likes to watch."

What Max liked to watch was left unsaid, as she lifted and glued her mouth to Ki's, eyes closed, nostrils flaring. Her fingers began gliding again, easing lower until they found the bulge in his groin and traveled its swollen length. She made a whimpering sound in her throat, and Ki held her tightly, sensing she was moist with anticipation as she traced the column of his erection.

Then her hands slid back to his waist. She fumbled eagerly, blindly with his rope belt, still not breaking the kiss. Ki was about to, so he could untie the belt for her, only to feel her nimble fingers prying the knot apart. As the rope ends fell dangling, she finished her kiss and stepped back a pace, her eyes sultry-lidded and sparking while she knelt and unbuttoned his fly.

"I knew it," she murmured as his tumescent flesh sprang

87

free. Wrenching down his jeans, she used both hands to grasp his shaft. "I knew it when I saw it soft this morning..." Licking her lips and leaning forward, her pink tongue fluting out for one exploratory taste, she fitted her mouth over the silky crown.

Responsively, Ki arched his hips, his eyes flaring when her tongue went into action. His thighs began to move in rhythm to her bobbing face, even as his hands tried to still her head and he gasped out, "Whoa a minute. Let me get my clothes off."

"Oh, all right," she said in a muffled voice. Stopping, she withdrew and sat back on her heels, looking up at him with deep eyes, smoky and mysterious. She smiled. "Well, hurry it up."

Ki shrugged off his vest and started yanking his shirt over his head. He still had it on by the arms, when Honora scrambled upright, flashed him another, more taunting smile, and darted giggling for the bank. "Last one in is a rotten egg!" she cried.

It took Ki less than five seconds to strip off his jeans and slippers, but by then Honora had dived gracefully from the edge. Dashing after her, Ki was in time to see only her firm buttocks and legs slicing into the pool, and, without pausing, he sailed in pursuit, hitting the water cleanly just as Honora surfaced.

She greeted Ki when he came up by dunking him back under. Twisting free of her headhold, he grabbed her ankles and dragged her down with him, where she slipped loose and sank deeper in a tight roll, brushing Ki as she rose out of it, giving him a quick kiss and a feel while thrusting by. Ki kicked after to repay her in kind, hearing her gasp as he broke surface alongside, with his hands cupping her breasts and squeezing them gently.

Their cavorting continued, playful yet erotic. They were both good swimmers, Ki agile and adept, and Honora a nude nymph with the grace of a seal. She was also passionately hot, as hot as the tantalizing feel of her lips and tongue when she swam between Ki's legs and guided his hardening length into her mouth.

Splashing, paddling, Ki tried to keep them from drowning as she tightened her lips and began sucking in earnest, her one hand stroking him while her other stroked the water. Her very awkwardness sent ecstatic sensations coursing through his loins, and when she relesed her clasp to draw air, he turned rolling and drew her close in a head-to-foot embrace. His fingers moved compulsively, spreading tenderly over her buttocks and dipping between her legs. Her thighs slackened, widening to allow him access, and he sank his mouth into her delta, lips and tongue delving between her soft curls and laving along her sensitive mound. Honora shuddered and gripped him by the hips, pulling him closer while she bobbed her mouth back and forth along his throbbing erection.

Then, without warning, she let go and kicked free. Uncaring, they'd drifted along to where they were near the pool's outlet, and Honora, after gesturing to Ki, swam toward the two big rocks. Ki followed, coming to the waist-deep shallows by the rocks and seeing her standing between them as if daring him to come get her.

Ki advanced, accepting her challenge.

Smiling expectantly, Honora crooked her arms on the flanking rocks, squatted down and thrust her legs straight out. She floated there at the channel entrance, braced by her arms, the outflow surging around her and spraying her upper body with beads of water.

When Ki got within range, she began kicking water, Ki took all that splashing for only as long as it took to grab her legs. Spreading them, he waded up between her thighs until his erection was spearing the crease of her splayed loins. Honora looked down at her impalement, Ki guiding with his hand until he was firmly locked sliding up inside her.

"Ahhh . . ." she cooed rapturously. She swung her arms, wrapping her legs around his waist and driving his hard male lance deeper into her sheath. She continued watching, swinging to match Ki's tempo as he pumped steadily, swiftly, her moist inner flesh clinging tenaciously to him, sending constant rippling sensations through them both.

Ki clenched his buttocks, thrusting his hips forward until she contained the whole of his girth in her milking loins. Her head sagged forward, then was flung back in arousal, her mouth open and gasping, her eyes viewing glassily, her long ebony hair swaying and brushing down between their tempestuous bodies. He toyed with her jiggling breasts, drilling faster into her pliant flesh while she strained to keep pace, her wide-split thighs hammering his pelvis, her legs embracing him with her knees bent waist-high and her feet crossed and drumming against his buttocks.

Ki could feel himself growing and expanding inside her, till he almost feared he'd explode from the exquisite pleasure building in his groin. And he could sense as well that Honora was also nearing her completion, as she gripped him ever tighter and moved more frantically against him, reveling in his harsh skewering thrusts.

"Now, Ki, now!" she pleaded, urging him on with the pummeling of her heels. Then she cried out shrilly, loud and piercing, uncaring if it brought anyone running from the road to her rescue. Ki didn't give a damn either, ejaculating violently into her loins. Shuddering, she orgasmed spasmodically with the beat of his pulsating spurts, arching forward to kiss him, deliriously flinging her arms tightly around his neck.

Her impulsive hug caught Ki off guard, and without the support of her arms bracing against the rocks, she was a top-heavy weight pulling him off balance. The funneling water pushed, its rapid flow sweeping his feet out from under him, and he toppled forward with Honora in an ungainly splash. Floundering and churning, still screwed tightly together, they were helpless to do more than hang onto each other as the current bowled them through the rocks and spewed them out into the creek, where they tumbled, bumpily disentangling, to a flopping halt.

On rubbery legs they staggered to dry ground, Honora coughing water and gurgling with laughter. "Sorry, I got carried away."

Ki stood panting. "Y'mean this isn't what usually happens?"

"Maybe to you, not to me. Roger isn't much for sporting." She touched Ki's chest with caressing fingers. "But Roger's never done a mean or dishonest thing in his life. If he's alive, find him for me. If he's dead, clear his name. In the meanwhile..."

"Meanwhile, it's time we should be going."

"I don't want to. Marie'll be hysterical, and Juan'll be mad at me for sending him out on that wild goose chase. Well, I had to think of *some* excuse, when Papa said Juan was leaving with you."

One look at her impish smile, her taut breasts and damply gleaming loins, and Ki realized he'd better act fast before she tricked him into even more hot water. Grabbing Honora by the hand, he launched her along as he headed strolling back to the clearing.

"Must you always have your way?" she snapped.

Ki didn't reply, but felt the protest was ironic coming from her.

"Naturally, you must. You have that strength, crushing, overpowering, virile..." Her voice was low, oddly breathless. A shiver passed through her and she dug in her heels, balking until Ki paused turning—then abruptly pressing in tightly, yearningly against him, her free hand fastening around his neck.

Ki felt the seething sensuality of her lips, and heard the teasing mockery in her voice when she drew back. "There. I just wanted to give you a sample of what you'll be missing."

Chapter 8

Finally arriving in Estero, Ki went directly to Indianhead and located the dockmaster checking manifests on the wharf. The dockmaster was in good humor, and queried by Ki, proved well informed about his regular clientele. He thought highly of them.

"Not well versed on Chadwick, though. Not my customer, and those that he takes over cease being mine, too. Sure, I ask him how he ships and what's his cost, but he avoids saying."

"That figures. What else do you know about Chadwick?"

"Well, he came here rich'n big, Ki, and o'er a year or so grown richer'n bigger. Grown ambitious, too, and's running for commissioner promising law'n order, and mostly what he wants, he gets. May vote for him myself, crime being so high, not that I care for his roughshod ways, or those toughs he hires to help him keep what he got. Though some ain't so tough, from what I hear tell happened this morning." The dockmaster winked broadly at Ki. "But watch out, the Roundheeler is port for Chadwick's crew, *all* of 'em."

"Is that bad?" Ki asked, mock-innocent. "Why, you make it sound so popular, I might have to visit just to pay my respects."

The dockmaster's laugh was deep and hearty.

When Ki left, he returned to the townside of the warehouse, where he retrieved his horse and started along a street of dowdy shops and cheap saloons. He stopped briefly in each, hoping to learn more. As this was the dull afternoon hour before the flurry of evening trade, he found the proprietors, bored and logy, were readily drawn into conversation.

By the time Ki had worked his way to the plaza, his general impression was that the townsfolk, like the dockmaster, supported Chadwick over crime. Those who disliked Chadwick, perhaps with good cause, were cautiously vague in voicing reasons and opinions. In specific information, Ki gleaned nothing new, nothing of value.

But the street was merely the preliminary leading up to the main bout—the Roundheeler. Ki went through its swinging doors into a large smoky room cool with wetted sawdust and crowded with patrons at tables and the bar. A few card games were going on at the rear, and the smell of Mexican cooking mingled with the familiar damp odors of the saloon.

Heading for the bar, Ki felt a tense, almost expectant hush grip the gathering, as if he were their long-awaited guest of honor. Yet he didn't recognize any of them, save for Damrow and Sheriff Dexter, who stood grouped at the bar with a stranger. Damrow's shirt bulged from chest-wound bandages, and his eyes stared with truculent hatred when he spotted Ki. The sheriff tried to put up a brave front, but regarded Ki with jittery apprehension. The stranger was about Ki's age, with features too flat-planed and a build too angular to be spoken of as handsome, and had frosty blue eyes which glanced once at Ki, then shifted indifferently away.

Ki's immediate aim was to nurse a beer. Just his presence was obviously disturbing, and he figured by lingering, he might churn things more. It was a good way to provoke a careless word, a reckless act, to force up the big stuff lying hidden underneath. It was also a good way to get killed.

94

Damrow was first to react rashly. Still goaded from the brawl, he shrugged off the sheriff's placating hand and stomped pugnaciously toward Ki. "So y'think you can waltz in here for a drink," he challenged when they met. "Well, slant-eyes, have mine."

He threw the contents of his whiskey glass squarely in Ki's face. As Ki flung up a shielding arm instinctively, Damrow cursed and grabbed for his pistol. But at the same instant, Ki lunged forward and caught the bald rowdy's gunwrist before the weapon was half out of its holster. He wrenched violently, ripping the pistol up and loose, sending it clattering to the floor. Then, with his one hand still vised around Damrow's wrist, Ki brought his shielding arm swinging down, his stiff-knuckled fist punching a swift tattoo in Damrow's shocked eyes and already puffed nose.

Yowling, Damrow blundered back against the bar, where the stranger grabbed his arm, restraining him. Ki stood alert anyway, daubing his watering, liquor-stung eyes with his sleeve. The sheriff stepped to pick up the pistol, which he handed back to Damrow with growling advice: "Take it and go cool off someplace, yuh idjit."

Damrow wiped his battered face with a blunt hand, holstered his pistol and left the saloon without a backward glance. Watching him leave from the corner of his eye, Ki went over to the sheriff, who'd motioned for Ki to join him a little further along the bar.

"Suppose you have that drink on me," the sheriff offered.

Ki nodded, smiling thinly, feeling wary yet intrigued.

"My way of gettin' you to talk with me," the sheriff said as two whiskeys were set up. "I mean, maybe I've got the wrong slant on things twixt Chadwick and them farmers like Mellon."

"Could be," Ki hedged. "How've you seen it?"

"Haven't been, that's just it, I've turned my eye. Figured

95

when the judge orders me to serve papers, I gotta serve 'em and tain't my business to say what's right or wrong in such matters."

"And naturally you have to think of votes, too."

"Well, uh, naturally." Sheriff Dexter cleared his throat and was peering into the depths of his drink when the stranger walked past. The stranger was adjusting his battered hat on his pale auburn hair and paid no attention to Ki or anyone else as he went out the swinging doors.

"But after I got back to town this afternoon, I got handed some papers that rattled me to my hocks," the sheriff continued. "They have to do with the note Chadwick's holding agin Mellon."

"Yeah? What exactly?"

"You oughta see 'em. Too plumb complicated for me to explain quick, and..." The sheriff glanced around worriedly, his voice lowering. "And if Chadwick knew I was spilling this, he'd never forgive me. Frankly, I want to win the next election, for I reckon he'll be voted commissioner."

"Provided he's still alive and kicking."

"Right, you got it." The sheriff nodded earnestly. "You can't blame a guy for wishin' to be on the safe side, now can you?"

"No, maybe not. Where're these papers?"

"At my office. You game to goin' there?"

Ki grinned again. "Sure . . . if you lead the way."

They finished their drinks and left, Ki trailing the sheriff closely. The sheriff might possibly be trying to lure him into a trap, but Ki didn't spot any of Chadwick's gunnies, not even Damrow, hanging about outside the saloon or around the plaza. He did see some fearful respect in Sheriff Dexter's washed-out eyes, and the lawdog might actually be wanting to go along with both factions.

Still, Ki didn't trust the sheriff and stayed close so that an ambusher would have difficulty getting a bead on him while they crossed to the small jail and office. Through the open door, a lighted lamp on the sheriff's desk showed that the office was empty. A barred gate cut the cellblock off from the office; it was shut, and no prisoners could be glimpsed in the block.

Sheriff Dexter went in first. After a swift check behind and aside, Ki stepped into the office and moved to keep the sheriff in sight, as the sheriff stooped, unlocking a drawer and taking out a sheaf of legal documents. Ki reached to take them—

And abruptly he recoiled, pivoting, finding himself staring into the muzzle of a black-stocked Colt Peacemaker. It was being gripped in the steady hand of a man who'd bobbed up from behind Sheriff Dexter's office—a man Ki recognized instantly as the disinterested stranger in the saloon.

Ki would've taken his chance, lashing out to disarm and escape, except for one thing. In his split-second glimpse, he recognized the California State Marshal's badge now pinned to the man's blue shirt. Oh, this was a trap, all right—one being planned for later, perhaps, but sprung at first opportunity, the sheriff delaying him with conversation to allow time for it to be set. Yet he hadn't done anything to justify legal arrest, and Ki was not about to start by maiming, possibly killing, a state officer.

The moment to resist gone by, Ki raised his hands.

"Smart o' you," the man said. "I'd have shot you happily, Sam Choy, for your dirty murder of Folsom Prison guard Hayward."

"You're mistaken. My name is Ki, and—"

"Cover Choy good, Dexter," the marshal snapped. "Choy, put your arms behind you." As Ki obeyed, feeling handcuffs being snapped tight on his wrists, the officer declared, "I, State Marshal Erik Veblin, hereby charge Sam Choy and detain him in custody."

"Better let me talk, Veblin, before you—"

"First read that," Veblin said. Having stepped back, redrawing his Colt, he used his left hand to toss a yellow paper open on the desk. It was a telegram, dispatched from Estero to the marshal's office in Stockton—where Veblin must be stationed, Ki presumed—and it said: SAM BIGAXE CHOY HIDING LOCALLY UNDER NAME KI. HAVE EVIDENCE, WILL WATCH HIS MOVEMENTS WHILE AWAITING YOUR ARRIVAL. It was signed: LESTER DEXTER, SHERIFF.

Ki gave the sheriff a savage glance, as Marshal Veblin continued, "I didn't know Hayward personally, but understand he'd an ailing wife and four kids. How you got ahold of one of your Tong hatchets to brain him with is still a mystery, but ain't no question your year of freedom is up, and you're goin' back to prison, this time to swing. Ain't no question you're you, too. You match the description too good, bein' so tall for an Oriental and so forth, even if you have shaved your beard and cut off your pigtail. Hayward's watch found in your room clinches it."

"In my room?"

"The hotel room where you slept last night. Must've overlooked it, and the maid there turned it in to Sheriff Dexter."

"Marshal, I never lost any watch or killed any prison guard. I never heard of Sam Choy. And I'm part Japanese, not Chinese!"

"He's one of them slick liars," Sheriff Dexter snarled. "Well, coolin' the night in my jug will take him down a notch."

"P'raps, Sheriff, but we're leaving right now."

"But you can't! He's gotta stay, er, I mean it'll be dark by time you reach Sacramento, and Choy's a wily bastard."

"Sure, that's why I ain't taking him the direct way. I'm going the longer way and holding him for the night at Stockton."

98

"I still say think again, Marshal," Sheriff Dexter argued. "Choy's got some salty-dog pals living upriver, and they'll shoot it out with you if they learn you're taking him in thataway."

"You'll eat dirt for this," Ki promised the sheriff, and turned grave-eyed to Veblin. "I've met a few folks here, but the only person who can prove I'm truly Ki, not Sam Choy, may be in Sacramento or on her way here. I'm not sure I can contact her."

"You'll get your chance. That's the law, and I believe in the law." Veblin prodded Ki with his revolver. "Now move, Choy."

With bitter amusement Ki could feel eyes watching him from doors and windows as he was taken outside to his horse. Already the plaza knew and soon the whole town would know of his arrest, the news no doubt being spread as preparation for a convenient lynching tonight. Leaving now stopped any such jail raid, but the talk would continue and, Ki hoped, be heard by Juan if and when the old farmhand arrived.

The bay gelding bit the sheriff, who was trying to hold it steady while Veblin propped Ki asaddle. A long rawhide thong was wrapped through Ki's handcuffs and tied to the saddlehorn, and a lariat was attached to a bridle ring so that the marshal could lead Ki's horse while riding his own, a long-legged buckskin.

A disgusted Sheriff Dexter was rubbing his nipped shoulder as the lawman and his prisoner headed north out of the plaza. Veblin kept checking warily around him, frequently glancing back at Ki, determined that the escaped murderer Sam Choy would not escape him. As insurance he'd looped shellbelts over his saddlehorn, so spare ammunition would be within easy reach for his revolver and the double-barrel shotgun in his saddle scabbard.

At the north edge of town, the trail to Stockton passed over a long, rickety bridge. It was more like a high causeway, built above floodstage over a wide, brackish slough that was fed by the river. The slough was now a marshflat of cattails and gumbo—the sort that could have pockets of quickmud just as deadly, Ki knew, as quicksand—but he also surmised that come winter weather and floods, the slough would fill rising till it resembled an estuary, the basis of the town's Spanish name, Estero.

From then on, the trail stayed vaguely parallel to the San Joaquin, straying with the pitch of the land through rolling hills and river-nourished growths of trees and brush.

Veblin didn't talk much, and Ki didn't want to much, either. The marshal had a bulldog tenacity, and what Ki wanted to say, he refused to hear, absolutely convinced his captive was an escaped convict and brutal killer. But his actions told Ki he was honest and would try to make up for his mistake when he eventually learned the truth.

The problem was what would happen in the meantime . . .

Late afternoon was upon them when, rounding an overgrown clay cut, Veblin glanced at Ki and abruptly jerked his buckskin to a halt. Craning, Ki saw where Veblin was staring past him at a group of riders galloping toward them. There were upwards of a dozen in the van with perhaps more behind in the dust clouds.

Veblin swore, "If they're your pals, coming to—"

"Not mine," Ki interrupted caustically. "They're your friends, or can't you make out the sheriff along with Fenton Chadwick in the center. They must've gathered fast after we left."

"Why? Where's Chadwick fit in?"

"It's his show. You've been used, Marshal, to help prove their claim I'm Choy and add credence to a lynch mob, say, to hang me."

"I won't let nobody take you, friend or foe." Hastily Veblin snatched up his shotgun and cocked both triggers. "And I sure's hell ain't gonna allow nobody to string up one of my prisoners."

"They won't, not now. Now they'll shoot us both down and call it a tragic escape attempt. And you can't stop them, not alone."

Veblin looked shaken. "If I let you loose and lend you a gun, will you promise to go on back with me—assumin' we can?"

"All right. If you're willing to risk my word, you've got it."

"I'm willin'. I'd soon's die as lose a prisoner," Veblin said, quickly releasing Ki, then handing over his revolver and a cartridge belt. Ki accepted them, for though he disliked firearms as a rule, the long-range stopping power of a .45 Peacemaker would be an asset. Plus, it let Ki keep his knives and *shuriken* in reserve, hidden from the marshal who'd likely confiscate them on sight, more positive than ever that Ki was the hatchet-wielding Sam Choy.

The riders, pointing at the dusty pair stopped in the trail, sharpened their clip as if fearing their quarry would try to race away. They needn't have worried; both the gelding and the buckskin were jaded after day-long use, and both Ki and Veblin realized it.

Ki buckled on the shellbelt and was flexing circulation back into his fingers when Chadwick and Sheriff Dexter, surrounded by their men, squewed to a halt. The tubular eyes of Veblin's shotgun, loaded with buckshot, stared at them, and they were careful to sit just past its range, some twenty-five yards, before making any play.

"Hi, you!" the sheriff yelled. "Been chasin' you almost since you left, Veblin, for the return of that maddog prisoner of mine."

101

"Well, you can chase yourselves right back to Estero," the marshal retorted. "You wired to come get Choy, and got him I have."

"But see here," Chadwick countered, waving a white document. "This's a warrant for Choy's arrest. You must turn him over to us."

"The state charge against him for jailbreak and murder has to be prior to any of yours, so it takes precedence," Veblin replied. "Choy is in my custody and'll be delivered safely to face trial."

"That's foolish," the sheriff called. "A waste of time."

"That's the law that you've sworn to uphold!"

"Sheriff Dexter certainly has and's pledged to see Choy gets a fair hearing," Chadwick replied pompously. "Tell you what, I'll lay double the reward on Choy, here'n now. Save you lots of trouble, and surely the slain guard's family could use the extra money."

Ki, holding the revolver behind him as though his hands were still cuffed, smiled ferally when he heard Chadwick's ill-disguised bribe. As he figured, Veblin was as pigheaded about honor as he was about everything else and was turning beet-red with indignation.

"Why, you dirty cuss!" the marshal roared. "I oughta pepper you with buckshot here'n now. You can't buy me. Now, keep away."

Chadwick leaned to confer with the sheriff and a couple of other riders in front, while stragglers from the so-called posse kept arriving to join the main party. After a lengthy moment, Chadwick said to Veblin, "Very well, Marshal, we'll pack it in."

Veblin, grumbling, shifted frontward in his saddle.

Ki hissed, "Watch out, you're putting your back to them."

"My eyes ain't," Veblin responded in a sidelong whisper.

Chadwick was motioning his riders off to the trail's shoulders as if ordering them to turn around. A line of them led by Sheriff Dexter was the first to swing aside—and the first to dig in their spurs and rush parallel to the trail, seeking to riddle the defenseless prisoner and back-shoot the marshal before he grew aware.

But Ki, whipping out his concealed revolver, and Veblin, alertly whirling his mount, turned the attack on the attackers. A split-second before the riders opened fire, they began shooting. Then bullets were blazing close around them, aimed poorly and triggered erratically by the startled, suddenly disorganized riders.

Chadwick began firing from down the trail, bellowing orders above the din. He made no attempt to join the charge, but swung out of the saddle to take cover behind his mount, protected from Ki and Velbin by his men.

Much as Ki would've liked to grab Chadwick, there was too much else to attract his attention. Already a second wave of riders was dashing to overrun him and the marshal, to down them by sheer weight of numbers. The blasts from Veblin's twin barrels, hurling spreading buck, combined with the belching revolver growing hot in Ki's fist, cut a wide swath in the galloping horde and managed to rout many of them. Others died and fell from their horses, or shrieked and slumped badly wounded to their leathers, or were thrown, sometimes pinned, when their mounts collapsed stricken with lead.

The leaders, including a miraculously unscathed Sheriff Dexter, veered out across the field opposite the clay cut, their parting shots sprouting dust and shale. The revolver and shotgun blasted again and again, hounding the riders as all of them, even Chadwick, tore for a grove of trees across the field.

"They're gone but I bet not for good," Ki said, lowering the Colt. "They'll rally and come back vengeful and plenty careful."

Veblin, snapping shut his freshly loaded shotgun, regarded the rent in his shirt sleeve where a bullet had furrowed along his forearm, then nodded. "A-men. Let's move out before they do."

Wheeling their horses uptrail, they spurted around the rest of the bend. To their dismay, they saw that the trail beyond the overgrown cut formed a straightaway through a flat tableland. For miles there were no trees, no bare rock formations to break it, only short, brown grasses curling low to the dry ground.

"We'll be sitting ducks out there without cover," Veblin said. "C'mon, leastwise I know my way around here a little bit."

Ki followed the marshal off the trail and up the cutbank, along what appeared to be a seldom used animal path. They climbed to the crest of the steep rise, where they dismounted and led their horses in among some sheltering rocks and foliage. From this vantage, they could rake the exposed trail below with gunfire—

As Chadwick's men soon discovered. Contrary to Ki's opinion, the regrouped posse came avenging but overeager, riding headstrong around the bend into a salvo of concentrated lead. Stymied by the ambush, they abandoned their dead and wounded as they had before and hastily retreated back behind the curve, howling their baffled fury. Then, at Chadwick's wrathful direction, they started circling around. Every so often, the two in the rocks above could catch glimpses of them, keeping low and out of easy range, as they stealthily worked higher and across to surround the pair in crossfire.

Ki said, "About time to move out again, don't you think."

"Uh-huh. See that patch of trees behind us? Let's go."

They beat the enemy to it, again tying their horses and making a short stand, disrupting the now dismounted riders with another surprise barrage before scrambling to yet another position. The afternoon waned into evening, and sunset faded into dusk, yet still they were forced to fight and run, managing to hold off the stubborn assaults with a series of skillful ploys and volleyed counterattacks. And though they were gradually wearing down the overwhelming odds, they kept being shoved farther southward, back toward Estero, never quite able to shake free and head for safety.

It was not until the full darkness of night that they finally succeeded in eluding their pursuers. They hid in a black wedge of trees, crouching motionless, straining weary senses, long after they no longer heard Chadwick's men call out to one another.

"We hafta make our break," Veblin muttered at last, eyes red-rimmed. "If we don't, I swear I'll fall asleep."

Ki nodded, also tired, and unbuckled the shellbelt. "Here, Marshal, I gave you my word you'd get your gun and me back."

Veblin waved the weaponry aside. "Stockton's soon enough."

Cautiously they hiked down to where they could mount. Then, occasionally silhouetted by hazy moonlight, they rode north in a circuitous route cross-country, avoiding fields and similar expanses, and having no intention of trusting open trails. Hour after hour they squirreled through brush and rocky terrain, Veblin familiar enough with the area to lead the way, Ki following armed and unshackled, fully trusted by the marshal after their baptism by fire.

They entered Stockton in the cool of early morn and jogged bedraggled on limping horses along the dusty main street. The town was like Estero, only more of it, but at this hour was as equally closed down and quiet. There were lamps lit in the sheriff's office and marshal's substation, which were housed together with a jail in a brick building; the structure occupied one corner of the main square which, like Estero's plaza, served as the central core for the town. Yet unlike Estero, Ki sensed no danger in Stockton, no sign of Chadwick other than a few election posters propped in some shop windows or tacked to fences.

Dismounting at the substation entrance, Veblin looked chagrined as he took his shellbelt and holstered revolver, then recuffed Ki's hands behind him. "Sorry, Choy, but rules are rules."

Inside, Ki was quickly booked and lodged in an empty cell. Veblin hesitated after locking the cell door, blinking haggardly at the man who had sided him so far, through so much. "I don't savvy it, and I'm too wrung out to try," he sighed. "All I know is I wish you weren't Sam Choy. I'll hate to hear of your hanging."

Ki responded with a faint smile and stretched out exhausted on the steel bunk. The marshal was still sure that he had collared the right man, and Ki had long since given up arguing the point.

★

Chapter 9

Ki awoke with dawn seeping through the window.

After a while a tray of oatmeal and coffee was slid under his door. Shortly the jailor returned for the emptied bowl and cup, and Ki idled away the early morning, trying to digest his gluey breakfast. The cell was small and barren, containing only his bunk and a rancid slopbucket, and was of the sort designed for overnight drunks and those briefly en route to the big jail in Sacramento or regular prison. Ki was relieved when the jailer came again, unlocked the door, and told him to get hustling.

From the cellblock, Ki was ushered into a sparsely furnished office. Its walls were plastered with wanted posters, fly-specked and yellowing, six straight back chairs lined below them. In one corner a gun rack held several rifles and shotguns, and at the far end a scuffed rolltop desk set under unbarred windows.

At the desk hunched a lean-shouldered man, gray at the temples and weathered dry as an autumn leaf. Ki had noted the office door was enscribed, LT. GILES, and it didn't take much to reason this man was Lieutenant Giles, or that he was an officer superior to Marshal Veblin, who stood looking miserable over by the gun rack.

Seated in one of the straight back chairs was Jessie, who immediately rose when Ki entered. She was smiling warmly, yet her face was drawn, indicating her sleepless night of searching for him.

"Thank heavens," she said with a sigh. "When Juan reported you'd been arrested, I went straight to Estero. There wasn't a sign of you or that wretched sheriff, and if it hadn't been for all the gossip, I'd never have known which way you'd been taken. Even then, until I reached here, I've feared you'd been waylaid."

Before Ki could reply, Giles asked, "Are you sure, Miss Starbuck?"

"I'm positive, Lieutenant. He's Ki and always has been."

Veblin agonized as Giles turned to pin him with coldly irritated scrutiny. "Well, the evidence . . ." he faltered lamely.

"Nonsense! You blundered, Veblin. However, 'tis human to err," Giles allowed, giving the platitude as if he'd originated it. He turned to Ki. "I trust, sir, you're of divine disposition?"

Ki had to chuckle. "Nothing to forgive. Marshal Veblin was tricked with planted evidence, by a lawman he'd no reason to question. His duty appeared clear, and he did it well. He should be commended."

"Sheriff Dexter's to blame," Jessie added. "Go after him."

"I can't arrest him or anyone on unsubstantiated charges."

Ki shook his head. "Proof isn't easy to come by. The sheriff's in connivance with Fenton Chadwick, who's busy cheating folks out of their property. No, I can't back that up either. Chadwick seems to operate behind a screen of legality with lawyers and court orders and power politics and, of course, with the sheriff."

"Sounds bad." Giles thought for a moment. "Chadwick has a lot of influence in this section, and if he denied your accusations—I can't imagine he'd admit to them—he could throw considerable weight, perhaps even blacken our reputation before it was over. As it stands, it's a regrettable case of mistaken identity. Beyond that, it's local politics, in which our policy is not to interfere."

"We understand, Lieutenant. We'll get along fine on our

own." Jessie smiled, masking her disappointment. "Forget it, please."

"I can't forget," Veblin interjected bleakly. "I may've been set up, but I was a damn fool and Ki, I owe you my apology."

"It's okay, really. I just feel lucky we got through the way we did. Soon as we can, Jessie and I'll head back to Estero."

"If you don't mind, I want to tag along," Veblin offered. "I don't feel any more done with what's going on there than you do."

"Why, yes, do come with us," Jessie answered for Ki. For a moment, while responding, she studied Veblin's face. She saw an angular profile of stern features, prone to expressions of strong opinion, with shadowed resentment etched in his cool blue eyes. He'd been wronged, and she read in his gaze the determination to right that wrong. He was, she sensed, giving a silent challenge—and that in turn made him a challenge which intrigued her, though this was hardly the moment to pursue such an interest.

Ki, nodding agreement, asked Giles, "With your permission?"

The lieutenant leaned in his swivel chair. "A full-scale investigation might, as I say, backfire on us. But one marshal merely checking about . . ." He folded his hands on his stomach. "It could do Veblin some good, at that. It definitely would keep the nincompoop out of my sight, before I bust him down a rank!"

Veblin reddened, almost squirmed. "Thank you, sir."

After Ki and Veblin regained their horses at the substation's stable, Veblin restocked his saddlebags and tied a warbag at the cantle, and both men rejoined Jessie for the trek back to Estero.

White sun was baking the late morning sky, searing the trail and its surroundings with blazing light. So they chanced taking the trail, riding with shaded eyes sweeping the way ahead, aware of Chadwick's hostility, the danger of a dry-gulcher's slug. Yet save for a distant dust plume heading away in their direction, and infrequent travelers greeting them politely as they passed, the trailway south remained clear as far as they could detect.

As they went, they exchanged what little information they'd learned. Jessie told of her three brushes with death, starting at Mrs. Willabelle's dinner and ending with Virginia Arp's demise. Ki recounted the *Paiute* raid and what transpired since—though, like Jessie, he skipped the personal details—and explained how Sheriff Dexter used Veblin as a catspaw to do the arrest and make the charge seem bona fide, while Chadwick prudently kept out of sight.

"But Chadwick's fear of Starbuck prompted the frame," Ki concluded. "I'm sure of it, as sure as he planned for me to die in jail or, if that failed, for me'n Erik here to have a shoot-out, maybe a fatal accident, on the direct road back to Sacramento. When *that* failed, he expected his mob to run us down on this trail."

"Thank God you stuck by your guns, Marshal Veblin."

"Erik, Miss Starbuck. If Ki can call me Erik, you should."

"Jessie. Turnabout's fair play."

"All right, Jessie," he agreed, slightly abashed. "Shucks, I can't take your credit, I was just being my obstinate self. But I guess we fooled 'em when the showdown came, Ki armed with my pistol instead of in cuffs. What got me fooled, though, was that watch. Sam Choy stripped Hayward's body, so I reckon whoever had the watch to plant must be cahootin' with Choy. Or is Choy himself. Say, Ki, have you seen any other tall Orientals slinking about?"

Jessie almost laughed at the vexed look Ki gave the marshal. "Gunther Mellon would know," she said. "You ask him when we get to his farm, Erik, while Ki takes his choice

110

of ruffling the foreman by coming back or soothing the daughter for having left."

"Honeydew's carrying on, eh?" Ki sounded the way he felt, unimpressed. "Theatrics, mostly. She's not acted upset over Page missing, and they're to be married. Tino's done all the stewing, but then, he's in love with her, too, and possibly he's uptight, fretting that Roger Page will appear before he can romance her."

Veblin asked, "Well, who does the girl love?"

"Herself, with adventure running a close second."

"Don't be catty," Jessie rebuked amusedly, then sobered. "Perhaps Tino has cause to worry. Perhaps he killed Page to stop the marriage, or because he, not Page, has been spying for Chadwick. If goaded by enough ambition, he'd feel motivated to remove anyone in his way or whose death might help gain his ends."

"I've known situations like that before, only . . ." Veblin frowned dubiously. "Plugging her suitor is mighty drastic and a poor solution, if the girl ain't particularily adoring of either guy. And if the foreman's hoping to marry into the farm, it don't reason he'd deal with a crook who'd leave him nothing to inherit."

"No, and Tino strikes me as bedrock loyal," Ki said. "Still, he may be gullible enough to believe Chadwick, who'd promise anything. Chadwick's duping lots of folks and scaring others, and once he wins the election, he'll have the legal clout to ruin them all."

"I think it's worse, more imminent," Jessie said somberly. "Chadwick isn't waiting till he controls the county's machinery. The writer of Virginia Arp's message agrees with him that it's high time to clean up here and is sending extra men with a big surprise—"

She paused abruptly, alarming Ki. "What's wrong?"

"I could kick myself," Jessie snapped irritably. "Riding

into Stockton this morning, I noticed two big freight wagons and a crew of men leaving the dock area. I assumed they were teamsters hauling cargo. I must've been asleep! They're Chadwick's reinforcements escorting his secret weapon. They have to be: The size and number and timing fit too right not to be!" She pointed skyward at the dustrise, now roiling thicker and nearer as their faster speed gradually overtook it. "And that has to be them up ahead!"

Ki mused, "Now I know where Chadwick does his shipping." He said to Jessie, "What're you annoyed about? You spotted them and figured out who they are and where they're going."

"Yeah, and in time for us not to run into them unaware," Veblin grinned slyly. "Now we can follow and see what cooks."

It was slow following, the convoy ahead proceeding at a snail's pace, and the open stretches made it impossible to dog closely without being seen. Morning eased into afternoon, the sun waxing stronger as it arced in a sky blue and flawless, save for the grainy dust. They plodded on, gauging by the volume of dust the progress of the convoy. The day was well along when the dust ceased billowing and began to dissipate.

Jessie pulled up. "They've stopped."

"By the bridge over the slough, I'd judge," Veblin said.

"I wonder why..." Ki rubbed an earlobe thoughtfully. "If they park there long enough, maybe we can work in behind them."

"Probably be better edging around down along the river to the slough and catch 'em from aside," Veblin suggested. "The trail cuts in near the river real shortly, if you want to try."

They did, and presently Veblin led them angling through a scrubby copse to a bordering field. The field ran on a shallow incline to the river, now seasonally low, its water a torpid yellow green. Dipping to it, they let their horses set their own pace, for though the bank was wide, it was of loose rock and dried clay, fringed with briars and bind-weed.

For a seeming eternity they sidled alongside water's edge, peering at the sky to catch sign of dust erupting afresh. Now and then they could glimpse portions of the trail, but mostly it ran just a bit too far away or was hidden by contours and foliage from view. At last they perceived they were approaching the slough.

Before reaching its broad mouth, they dismounted and anchored their horses' reins under rocks, gratified by the continuing lack of dust. Then, taking binoculars from their saddlebags, they crept forward to where the river gently curved to form the bay of the slough. From there it was a crawl, a muddy struggle through prickly grasses and inter-woven plants that flourished along with swarms of carniv-orous insects in the silt and brackish water.

When they advanced as far as they dared, they hunkered low in a patch of skunk cabbage and surveyed the convoy, which was halted on their side of the bridge, across from Estero.

Dust clogged the iron-sheathed wheels of two monster freight wagons, Conestoga in style but lacking the usual bowed wagon cover. Damp dust coated their teams of exhausted mules, and more dust blanketed the large, canvas-draped crates in their bed.

"Big surprise, you ain't a-kiddin'," Veblin said to Jessie. "What d'you figure is in them boxes that Chadwick's waiting for?"

"I don't know. I had a notion it might be explosives."

"Throwing bombs means running in close, and Chad-wick's men haven't been crazy at making heroes and corpses of themselves." Ki shrugged. "Maybe these new ones he's getting are different."

If they were, they didn't show it. Sufficient were in view for Jessie to estimate the promised number of thirty were all there, and typical of the breed, they were taking the opportunity to laze gabbing, smoking, and drinking. Only a handful of men were seeming to work, busily engaged in poking around the bridge.

"Looks like they don't trust it," Ki remarked.

"That's funny," Veblin observed. "It's strong enough for full wagons, though it wobbles some when you go it at a gallop."

They watched, curious. The span was of wood planks nailed to long logs. In the center of the slough, on a flat rock rising above the swampy water, were thick timbers which supported the middle of the structure. These the five men acted concerned about.

And studying the five through her glasses, Jessie could make out the features and clothing of a man the others treated deferentially, like a boss. He was tall, thinned-down, wearing a military cap and a double-breasted tunic, and his face was scarred diagonally from his left eye corner to his brutish chin. It was a cut which had healed poorly, so that scar tissue stood out prominently against his protuberant eyes and flat, pale cheek.

"A Heidelberg student's saber slash, if I ever saw one," Jessie murmured grimly to herself. "The cartel has arrived."

Ki touched her shoulder. "Company's coming."

Shifting, Jessie now saw a group of riders loping across the bridge from Estero, led by a town-suited toad of a man and a lanky man wearing a star. Fenton Chadwick and Sheriff Dexter, unless she missed her guess. Hoarse shouts sounded, and shots of welcome were fired in the air as the two gangs joined forces.

After a few minutes the same five men and Chadwick peeled from the mingling throng and huddled in discussion. Then they inspected portions of the bridge, starting at the top and carefully working down the bank to its base, crossing on smaller stepping stones to the flat rock outcrop, where their conversation became more of a wrangling. The scar-faced man whipped out a knife and began stabbing the timbers, gesturing heatedly as he displayed gouged chunks of wood to Chadwick.

And now Jessie realized what was causing the convoy's delay. The main span depended upon those two central posts, and though they were a foot through and seemingly sturdy, they'd begun to rot from the slough's annual flooding. True, there was some lateral support from horizontal beams, but the two posts were all-important for carrying any sort of weight on the bridge. The scar-faced man had a right to worry and to refuse to risk it.

"They're testing the bridge, all right, and don't look happy with the verdict," Ki said. "That load must be too heavy."

"Then it'll stay on this side a good while," Veblin declared. "Only way to shore the supports is with long, big logs, and there aren't any long, big trees growing around here."

The thought of a delay was heartening, and Jessie continued viewing the men by the posts with determination to make the most of it. Getting Mellon and his friends to attack the convoy was one way to commit suicide. There were simply too many gunmen, and they'd have the wagons for cover. Getting the farmers prepared to defend themselves was another way, but according to Ki, they were already on alert, patrolling and guarding, armed to the teeth. Besides, defend against what? Chadwick had secrets, above all his big surprise, that must be uncovered first. Yet Chadwick would hardly trust anyone outside his gang, not any farmer and certainly not Ki, and definitely not a total stranger unless...

Unless he was expecting that stranger. Well, Chadwick

was expecting a lady messenger from Sacramento, and since Virginia Arps had never met him, it stood to reason she'd have been a stranger to him. But whatever lady delivered the letter would be the favored filly for a time. Perhaps for enough time.

"Listen," Jessie announced to Ki and Veblin, "I've thought up a scheme to get close to Chadwick." Briefly she explained it.

"What, alone?" Veblin was aghast. "Like a floozy?"

"Well, if you suppose you can look more like Virginia, be my guest. Personally, I can't conjure you in a wig and corset."

Reddening, Veblin shook his head. "They're a nasty lot, Jessie. Chadwick will toss you to them if he ever gets the least suspicious, and they'll kill you without a qualm."

"I realize that. I had a taste of their ways on my way here. But somebody has to find out Chadwick's strength and his plans, and the only somebody here who meets the specifications and has the letter is me. So me it is, and I won't waste time arguing."

"You're going now?" Ki asked, accepting her decision.

"Yes. I've a lot to do, and I want to get to Chadwick while he's still distracted by the bridge problem. Now, Ki, please tell Mellon and maybe a few others, but be discreet," she instructed. "If they see me riding with Chadwick, I don't want them jumping to the wrong conclusion, but I don't want the truth leaked back, either."

Ki nodded, smiling. "We may not even recognize you."

"If that's a compliment, thanks." She turned to leave.

"Jessie, wait, you can't—"

Pausing to look back, she squelched Veblin with a stare, but her parting words were for Ki. "Erik's sure a contrary soul. You seem to have a good effect on him, Ki. He needs calming down."

She wriggled away through the noxious growth, and Veblin, eyeing her undulating buttocks, let out a sigh of a man defeated.

"I don't care for this business—any of it," he told Ki morosely. "I can scent more trouble on the way, and when it does come it'll probably be an avalanche."

Chapter 10

After jogging back north along the river, Jessie cut east and then south in a wide sweep around the slough. To use the Stockton trail would've been simpler and brought her quicker to Chadwick at the convoy; yet it could've raised suspicions, she realized, it not being the route a messenger from Sacramento should be taking. Crossing the slough directly to Estero would've even been shorter, but she would've risked being spotted out there in the open and most likely bogged down in no time flat.

So she preferred to detour the slough, following no path, only her own vague sense of direction cross-country to intersect the Sacramento road. When finally her haphazard course ended at roadside, she had to ride along an intervening fenceline until she found a gap. Then, heading townward, she wondered how to look like a floozy, as Veblin had put it. She didn't travel with such costumes and warpaint and seriously doubted they'd be stocked in any outlying farm community like Estero. Well, if she couldn't gussy up, she'd have to bluff it. Perhaps that wouldn't be too terribly difficult; in every woman, even the nicest, there was a little bit of the whore.

It was not yet dark when she reached Estero in the reddening late afternoon sun. The stores were thriving and the hitchrails were packed, the cooler evening enticing shoppers out. Saloons, especially the Roundheeler, were crowded with Chadwick men, both his old hands and the new, who'd

118

crossed from the convoy with money burning their pockets and thirst parching their throats. Some of the new remained behind, Jessie perceived; a few were guarding the wagons, while others were laboring below the bridge. Distance and dusk prevented her from discerning their work, but she saw enough to spark dread within her—the dread that the delay would be far shorter than Veblin prophesied, a matter of hours instead of days.

She proceeded into the plaza and was angling toward the street leading to the bridge when she saw Sheriff Dexter striding toward his office. Spurring across to him, she called, "Sheriff? Do you know where I may find Mr. Chadwick? Can you take me to him?"

Stopping, the sheriff turned. "Can't, ma'am; he won't be pestered right now. P'raps later, like try tomorrow."

"But I've come from Sacramento with a message for him."

"Message from Sacra..." The sheriff blinked, as if something dawned on him. "I'll take it," he said, recovering. "Say, we've been looking for you, you're late. What's your handle, sweetie?"

"Virginia. That's good enough, isn't it?"

"Plenty good. I'll see Mr. Chadwick gets your message."

"Sorry. My boss said I was to hand it direct to him."

The sheriff regarded Jessie's set jaw and steady eyes and shrugged grudgingly. "Okay, okay. Tie up and follow me."

Jessie dismounted, dropping her reins over the rack in front of the sheriff's office, and trailed the lanky lawman through the plaza. This's a break, she thought; she'd passed the first test and now had an entry to Chadwick.

But Sheriff Dexter didn't take her across to the convoy, where she assumed Chadwick was still hanging about. Instead he went a couple of doors down a sidestreet, to a storefront whose window was freshly emblazoned: FENTON CHADWICK ELECTION COMMITTEE. Ushering her inside, he said, "Hold your bustle," and left by an inner hallway. The lamplit room, part of a vacated shop, was sparsely furnished, the biggest attraction being a wall-to-wall streamer reading: FOR COMMISSIONER: CHADWICK, THE PEOPLE'S CHOICE.

Soon the sheriff came beckoning and led Jessie through a hall to a large rear office fitted with chairs, desks, and a carpet. A wizened clerk with an eyeshade and ink-stained fingers was fiddling with a taper, lighting the gilt oil-lamps hanging from their chains.

At a larger desk sat a man in shirt sleeves, his suit jacket draped around the back of his swivel chair. He was leaning back watching Jessie as she followed the sheriff into the office, and was the stout, thin-lipped, pomade-haired frog she'd thought earlier to be Chadwick. Now she was convinced. His gray gaze was calculating, shrewd, indicating a sharp, albeit evil, mind. It took such a brain to run with the cartel and wield political power.

"Good evening," he said cordially. "You have a message?"

"For Mr. Chadwick, nobody else."

"That's me, m'dear."

"I ain't your dear, mister, and maybe you ain't Chadwick."

Chadwick frowned, but Sheriff Dexter, who was just leaving, let out a guffaw. "Looks like we got sent a prickly one this trip. Try Virginia; it's maybe her name." He shut the door after him.

Chadwick, regaining his composed smile, pointed at his desk. "See for yourself, er, Virginia. My mail, and other documents."

Still acting hard and suspicious, Jessie sifted cursorily through the litter of papers and chanced upon Gunther Mellon's loan note. She picked it up, the paper crackling as she held it to the light. "Pretty watermark," she commented and

120

tossed it back. "I'm satisfied. Don't hold it against me for being careful."

"Not at all. I admire caution in a woman."

Jessie took the folded envelope from her pocket and handed it to Chadwick, who swiftly opened it and read the letter. Then nodding, he stuck it in a desk drawer and looked again at Jessie.

"Well, it's overdue and after the fact, but nice to get anyway." Chadwick was plainly pleased. "Was there a hang-up along the way?"

"A couple of gents with fresh ideas, but nothing I couldn't handle by my lonesome," Jessie replied, slapping her holster. Her tone was a mixture of conceit and boasting, as she sought to account for her lack of bodyguards, while impressing herself on Chadwick. "I enjoy my work. You can count on me to deliver."

"I'm sure I can, Virginia. So please relay my sincerest thanks and assurances we'll strike at once before more opposition builds up or any authorities catch wind. Oh, yes, and that I'll have my area under control in time to prepare for spring sowing."

"Right." Hesitating, Jessie pondered how to press for more without proving herself ignorant of what she was supposed to know. Then figuring her best defense was to attack, she gambled saying: "I hope *you're* right, too. Frankly, patience is wearing thin up my way. Glad to help, mind you, but some're wondering why you haven't been able to bust a rabble of farmers with what you've already got."

"Faster said than done. They've mustered arms and ammo enough for a small war, and fighting scattered in their fields, it'd take a thousand more boys than I got to root them all out."

"Burn them out. You have been, haven't you?"

"Selectively. Up till now, like I say, finishing them in one

121

fell swoop has been impossible. I've had to pick them off one by one, which takes time and care. Raiding their farms and attacking the boats shipping their cargo are squeezing them bankrupt, but not overnight. Same for my legal maneuvers, the courts being ponderously slow. And right now they're harvesting the wheat, *my* wheat, and I'd hate to lose a fortune up in smoke. Mellon and his clodhopper pals have put a mighty big drain in my pocketbook."

"Well, you make sense to me, but I don't make the decisions."

"No, but you can pass along my promise of swift results. In the next couple of days, those farmers will get a surprise, a big surprise that'll drive them to Mellon's ranch. By then, Abe will've completed the warrants and other legal papers I need." Chadwick winked and thumbed toward the clerk, who was now hunched writing at the other desk. "He's a topnotch forger, Abe is."

"I see. You'll corner them with the weapon we sent."

"For that one big wipeout, yes. If they refuse forfeiture and arrest by our duly sworn officers, they'll be outlaws. If they get hurt or killed resisting us, it'll be their own fault."

There was a knock at the door, and Sheriff Dexter came in.

"What now, Lester?" Chadwick demanded impatiently.

"Linz is ready with his demonstration, okay?"

"Be right with you." Chadwick began closing the open desk drawer, saying to Jessie, "Y'know, watching this'd be something to deliver back to Sacramento. Want to take a walk and see?"

"Love to."

Chadwick didn't seem to hear. He'd stopped shutting the drawer and was frowning into it; then straightening, he stared fully, quizzically at her. "Say, have you got more for me?"

122

She looked down at herself. "How much more you need?"

"Another piece of paper for one, with a drawing on it."

"If it's not in the envelope, no. Is it vital?"

"Nothing that can't wait. It's of Miss Starbuck and her Chink crony, to identify them by." Chadwick's face tightened. "Starbuck! They're against us, worse'n a pack of marshals, with power and money galore!" He thrust the drawer closed and stood, calming as he slipped on his suit jacket. "Well, I already know what that bastard Ki looks like. He's a fugitive, and if he dares step foot back here, he'll be shot on sight. Same goes for that hussy he sides for aiding his escape or whatever."

"And all done to look legal," Jessie said, and perceiving an opening for another gamble, she scooped up Mellon's note again and added caustically, "For your sake, I sure hope their death reports are faked on better paper than this."

"Don't be absurd. That note'll stand up in any court."

"Not on paper unavailable six years ago, when this's dated."

"What? How can you tell the age of the paper?"

"The watermark." Jessie smiled disdainfully. "You should know that paper is branded, like a cow, and this one has the stamp of two crossed quills. So happens my late second husband's sister wrote me last Christmas on paper like this, saying it's a sample from the new mill starting up, where her two sons had gotten jobs."

"Chre-rist!" Chadwick roared, snatching the note away from Jessie and holding it to the light. "It's true!" He swung to face the clerk, his features a mask of fury. "You've ruined me, Abe, scribbling on this worthless paper! Nothing'll pass now, and what has will be reversed! All my time, all my efforts, and for what? For a long stretch in prison, that's what! You stupid imbecile!"

As he raged at the clerk, Chadwick darted his hand into his jacket pocket. The clerk may've been wizened but he

123

was game and apparently knew what the pocket contained. Barking an oath and scrambling upright, he snatched a long-bladed letter opener off his desk. His chair crashed back, the sheriff ducked, and Jessie shifted ready to draw. And Chadwick whipped out a stubby-barreled hideout gun and shot the clerk cleanly between the eyes.

The clerk shriveled in a heap, inky hands still clutching the letter opener, sightless eyes open, and emphasized by the black little puncture just above his bridge. No blood, no muss, and the fuss was now over, Chadwick retiring his smoking gun to his pocket, then stooping to pick up the note he'd let fall to the floor.

"Lester," he ordered, casually tearing the note into shreds, "get a couple of boys and a barrow, and plant ol' Abe in Boot Hill." Then flipping the shreds in the air, he turned to smile pleasantly at Jessie. "C'mon, Virginia, we don't want to keep Linz waiting."

The shreds fluttered like snowflakes over the body.

Jessie felt appalled as she accompanied Chadwick through the plaza to the bridge. His charming urbane manner was now firmly back in control, yet only moments before she'd witnessed how fast it could slip, how superficial it was and easy to prick. Under his thin coating of veneer, he was one of the most savage, insanely egotistical and blood-lusting enemies she had ever run up against.

Nonetheless, she had to play the role of a woman equally callous and jaded. Well, almost as. So strolling along with him she remarked, "I'm speaking out of turn, I know, but weren't you a mite hasty back there, downing your topnotch forger?"

"What I thought was first class, proved, thanks to you, to be a liability. All forgery is out now, due to Abe's bungling, for I can't have new claims questioned without risking ones already passed by the courts. No, Virginia, I'm an easygoing fellow at heart, but I believe in eliminating losses quickly as possible."

"Doesn't that leave you relying more on the election?"

"True, and on swift, brute force against holdouts like those farmers. Y'see, I use varied methods," he explained affably, "all combining into what I call my philosophy of terror. I expect to expand its application as I gain more political power."

Jessie shuddered inwardly and lapsed silent while they crossed the bridge. Dark had fallen by now, but approaching the other side, she could see by glow of numerous lamps and torches that her earlier dread had been well founded. Somewhere, somehow, stout trees had been located and felled—not as thick and tall as Veblin had figured necessary, no doubt, but the marshal was not a structural engineer like the scar-faced man most likely was. While some of the workers were hacking off limbs and chopping trunks into prescribed lengths, others were hauling the prepared logs down the bank, where more men were jamming them under the horizontal beams and lashing them to the main uprights.

Reaching the convoy, Jessie caught her first look at Chadwick's big surprise. Big it was, bulking massive on the ground behind the rear wagon; and surprise it was, a canvas cover fastened completely over it. As she and Chadwick approached, she also saw the wagon's tailgate down and heavy planks perched against the bed rail, indicating how, by means of ropes now lying about, the weapon had been dragged off. The scar-faced man was supervising the placements of chocks around its base to insure the brute did not move on its own. Finishing, he stood awaiting their arrival.

Despite its cover, Jessie had seen similar shaped outlines before and feared she recognized what it was. When the scar-faced man finally and with a grand flourish removed the cover, she knew she was right. It was an army field mortar. The mortar alone was no more than four feet long, but weighed over twelve hundred pounds due to being made of cast iron gun metal, and it was mounted on a carriage that weighed a good nine hundred itself.

The scar-faced man strutted over. "Magnificent, no?"

"By God, yes, Linz," Chadwick declared, beaming. "Will everything be ready so we can start action at tomorrow sunset?"

"Yes, sir. The bridge should be traversable by morning, in fact." Linz had a slight foreign accent, Jessie noted, and didn't seem prone to sprinkling his English with foreign expressions. "As for my baby, I always keep her prepared for campaigns. Just to show what she can do, watch that abandoned cabin over yonder."

Linz barked an order, and two men came trotting. Normally loading was a one man task, but two looked twice as impressive, so Jessie wasn't surprised when one hastened off while the other stayed and, at Linz's shouted command, fired the field mortar.

The booming discharge resounded over the landscape, and a small shock wave quivered the ground beneath them. Their gaze was focused on the cabin Linz had pointed out, derelict and tilted awry a fair quarter-mile across the slough. It erupted into the air, disappearing in a gushing spew of debris and soggy earth. When the discharge settled, the cabin was no longer there.

Jessie felt sick. Some of the men standing about began whooping hurrahs. Chadwick was chortling and slapped Linz on the back, and Linz was gloating as if his baby had given birth.

"It was luck, shooting a bull's-eye the first time," Linz said with feigned modesty. "But after a few more tries, a little practice, my artillerymen will be able to hit any target dead-on."

"Linz, I'm counting on you to do exactly that," Chadwick

said. "We'll blow the scum out of their crackerbarrel nests and everywhere else they try to dig in and hide, and exterminate them once'n for all." He was in high good humor and chuckled again as he turned to Jessie. "Well, Virginia? What do you think?"

Jessie managed a smile. "It's a fine idea, Mr. Chadwick."

"Fenton, m'dear. Are you staying over tonight?"

"If needed. I'm supposed to serve you best I can."

"Best way to serve me is to relax and serve yourself. My ranch isn't far, and you may as well eat'n drink and bed down comfy there. Tell you what, we'll go have dinner together."

Jessie nodded, forced to agree in her attempt to counter his vicious plot, and chilled to the bone at the prospect. Chadwick had not only accepted her as the messenger, but was now hinting she should deliver herself as well. Damn him, if he tried rutting with her, she vowed any climax would be to his life, not in his loins.

Shortly they were moseying along the Sacramento road, Chadwick pressing stirrup-to-stirrup and growing increasingly chummy. Jessie fended without offending, feeding his vanity to draw out more facts.

"I bet you're already preparing for the election after this," she said at one point. "Sacramento is, and means to support you."

"With such backing I might reach—ah!—the state senate."

"Or governor. No telling how high you could rise."

"Governor!" Chadwick, preening with the notion, made a deprecating gesture. "No, no, others would be better qualified."

"Not if you-know-who thinks you're best," Jessie replied, not knowing the who and hoping Chadwick would respond with a name.

Her hopes were dashed, Chadwick clamping his mouth

shut as they heard the swift hoofbeats of an oncoming horse. Caution prevailing, they veered off to the shoulder of the fence-hemmed road and sat motionless, hands tensed near their weapons.

The lone rider approached at a gallop, lashing his mount with his reins. When he drew close enough to discern his slack, chinless features, Chadwick stiffened in recognition and abruptly spurred out onto the roadway, yelling, "Webster! Hey, stop!"

Jessie launched following. Startled, the rider called Webster almost collided into them. He yanked frantically on his reins, his horse rearing high and pawing to a skittish halt.

"Jesus," Webster panted. "You scared me, boss."

"Looked more like you were riding scared. Bad news?"

"Good. We got that badge-toter, Marshal Veblin."

"You didn't, you couldn't. What'd he be doing here?"

"I dunno, but we did." Webster shrugged, still breathless. "At ol' man Lyden's farm. Was set to torch his barn, when Lyden caught on and let fly with a rifle from his kitchen window. Damrow plugged him, we went in his house to make sure, and Veblin showed up."

"Showed up how? Where'd he come out of, thin air?"

"From the Mellon fields, near's we tell, probably attracted by our gunfire. Put up a helluva tussle. Damrow liked to shoot him, natch. We held off, figured you'd maybe want a crack first. But we reckoned we'd better get more men to take Veblin to town. Feared Mellon's pack might be about, too, and try'n rescue him."

"Smart of you boys. Okay, round up some help at the saloon, but bring the marshal to my place and lock him on ice with the kid." Chadwick's gray eyes glowed malicious, his lips curved in a mirthless smirk as he turned to Jessie. "If ever I get to be governor, I'll see to it the marshals are changed. Only thing I'll keep is the name, maybe. Well, let's go. I'm hungry."

128

"My appetite's changed. Fenton, my second husband was killed by a marshal in San Diego," she said with biting venom. "Take me to this Veblin. I want to see him; I want to feast on marshal-meat."

"But Virginia, in a short while we'll be at my—"

"Now, not later." She wrenched her horse out, past Chadwick and Webster. "I can't wait," she called, as she spurted off.

"Females!" Chadwick snapped disgustedly. Leaving Webster to head for town, he tore after Jessie. "You damn well will wait," he bellowed, as she slowed to let him catch up. "You women are all alike, running away without knowing where you're going."

It was a half hour's journey. The roan was swift, and Chadwick was only a few jumps ahead of Jessie when they reached the yard of Lyden's farm. The house was a short, single-story "four-square" bungalow, too cramped for a family but pretty efficient for a bachelor or widower. An outhouse, shed, and barn loomed in shadowy relief, touched by faint moonlight and bordered by wheat fields. Lined in front of the house porch were ghostly figures of eight horses, not tied to the porch railing but left ground-reined and saddle-cinched in case, Jessie surmised, their riders inside the house had to beat a hasty retreat.

Rather than crowd in along the porch, Jessie and Chadwick went around to the rear stoop. Shouting, "Don't shoot the boss, boys, or you won't get paid next Friday," Chadwick opened the door.

Entering the kitchen behind Chadwick, Jessie saw Veblin slouched by a set of shelves, left of the rear door and in line with the entry into the front room. Sitting upright against the front of the cookstove was a man of about sixty, white-haired and in coveralls, who Jessie assumed must be Lyden. The farm's owner might've passed for merely resting adoze, if it weren't for one side of his head being missing, and his

129

brains being splattered all over the burner plate and upper bun warmer of the cook stove.

The cast iron stove filled the corner to the right of the east window, with the door in the center of the north wall. It took up much of the space in the small kitchen, and what it didn't, eight men did. They were all bleach-eyed jiggers, tight-mouthed and heavy-armed, wearing nondescript clothes and dusty boots—and the worst appeared to be a barrel-chested lout with a bald skull and a pug-ugly countenance messed uglier by recent fighting.

At the moment the bruiser looked happy, standing over Veblin as though relishing the marshal's having his hands tied behind him, his feet secured by cords. Dark floor stains, a mix of Lyden's and Veblin's blood, reflected wetly from the glow of lamplight.

"We kept him for you," the bald man growled when Chadwick came up. "We even softened him some for you. Damned I know why."

"Damned I know why he's here, Damrow. Do you?"

"Sure, to die."

"Marshals just don't float about, they're dispatched on assignments." Chadwick frowned thoughtfully. "I wonder..." He hunkered and grasped Veblin by the shoulder. "Talk, and you might live. Did Mellon or any of his lot ask help from you marshals?"

Veblin was groggy and slurred, "Who's Mellon?"

Chadwick shook him. "Tell me who sent for you."

"Nobody sent for me. I'm on vacation."

"Kick his teeth out," Damrow suggested.

"Better not, I need 'em to chew up jackasses."

Damrow snarled. "Are you insinuating I—"

"Pipe down, Damrow," Chadwick barked and then slapped Veblin twice across the face. "C'mon, talk! Why are you here?"

Veblin, already weakened by abuse, slumped moaning.

"He must've come for a farmer," another man insisted.

Propping Veblin, Chadwick demanded harshly, "For the last time, why? What's your reason? And where's Ki?"

"I . . . I dunno no Ki, neither."

"He's that sonuvabitch you took to Stockton, remember?"

"Oh, him. He's why I'm on vacation. Not Sam Choy . . ."

"Listen, boss," Damrow said, agitated. "Listen, say you're right. Say he got sent here in answer to their call. You ain't gettin' nowhere, and there's no time to lose! We gotta dump him!"

Veblin braced himself, determined to face death squarely. "You'll regret this," he said evenly, if thickly. "Eventually you'll pay dearly for the crimes you've committed in California."

"Shut up, you lawscum!" a third man snapped, kicking him.

They all cursed him then, and when Chadwick rose and stepped aside, they fell upon him with fists and gunbarrels. Veblin curled writhing helplessly, until finally he relaxed, battered unconscious.

Chapter 11

All this while, Jessie had been standing by the door, her expression of pleasure transfixed by her inner horror. Every fiber cried out to shoot Chadwick and as many men as her pistol had bullets, and then use her derringer to down a couple more. But if Veblin could take the torture and not crack, so must she.

"Great!" she now exclaimed, as Chadwick glanced her way. "When he comes to, do it again harder. I *hate* marshals."

"Want me to get some water, boss?" a gunnie asked.

"No, let him lie." Chadwick turned away. "If he wakes, fine. If he don't, he'll be easier to carry when Webster gets back."

The men began to loll around. Occasionally some would go outside to stretch and relieve themselves, but mostly they prowled indoors, rifling Lyden's belongings and talking stupidly.

Despite the gruesome corpse, Jessie remained in the kitchen to guard Veblin from being killed on the sly. She masked her watching by moving about, pausing by the entryway to check the front room and bedroom beyond; or take glimpses out the bullet-shattered window facing the barn, or out the east window overlooking the fields toward Mellon's; or chat companionably with the men who roamed in.

Although apparently relaxed, actually she was nervously

seeking means to save Veblin and herself. She had uncovered crucial information, hopefully enough to destroy Chadwick's menacing power, yet she could not abandon Veblin to certain death, not while there was any possibility of bringing him along. And each stroke of a minute cut that much off her slimming chances.

Twenty of those precious minutes passed. Once again Jessie paused by the doorway and saw Chadwick still conversing in the front room with a couple of his boys. There were sounds of two more in the bedroom, and three others were behind in the kitchen.

Things all looked much the same, except for Damrow kneeling at the front room's west window. He'd pulled the worn draperies shut around him, as if to avoid the room's feeble light; and though he was hidden down to his knees, Jessie could recognize him by his boots and broad pant legs. His cloaked outline suggested he was resting against the window sill, holding something to his shoulder.

Curious, Jessie went back to the west kitchen window. Peering at the same scene Damrow was viewing, she shielded her eyes from the kitchen's lampglow, and after a moment she glimpsed the answer. A man had just crept from the wheat and in a flash had sprinted over to vanish behind a clump of brush.

She blinked, struck by how the man resembled Gunther Mellon. Then, for a split-second, a couple more faces appeared in the field, one looking much like Tino's, and the other damn well unmistakably being Ki's. Electrified, Jessie suddenly realized that they'd miss Veblin and go hunting him, and finding Lyden's house lined with horses and filled with Chadwick men taking leaks, they'd—

She had to act, instantly. For a breath Jessie considered firing a shot, to warn their sneak attack hadn't been sneaky enough. But her shot might mistakenly signal them into rushing, and anyway, it wouldn't alert them as to where exactly their peril lay.

Damrow, that's where. The thing he was shouldering had to be a rifle, she realized as she darted for the inner entryway. And reaching the entryway door, she saw the draperies rippling. Damrow was shifting to draw a bead, his motions precise, easy to read now that she knew what to look for. His target was moving fast, as though crossing open yard to get nearer, blinded by the shrouding drapes from spotting Damrow aiming out the window.

She had to shoot. Her custom .38 blurred from the speed of her frantic draw, then bucked as she triggered lead into the drapes. Damrow howled, shuddering from the impact. His rifle seemed to echo her shot and drown his agonized cry. Reflexively he grabbed, as if in dying he wished to brake his lurching fall, his hands clutching the drapes and ripping them loose. They dropped, rod and all, while he collapsed ungainly on the floor, his crouched legs still bent under him, the draperies covering over him like a rumpled body shroud.

As the drapes came tumbling, Jessie noticed Damrow's rifle siding off the sill to the ground outside. And yonder she glimpsed Mellon retreating in a zigzag to the wheat. But mainly her attention focused on the front room, acutely aware that she had herself and the helpless, comatose marshal yet to extricate.

Fenton Chadwick and the pair with him were leaping into action after their initial shock, while the two in the bedroom were rushing out. Chadwick was turning even as Damrow began toppling, and seeing Jessie in the doorway with her revolver lancing smoke, he shouted above her reverberating gunshot, "God, she drilled Damrow! Get the bitch; she's a wrongo!"

His raging words were lost in a barrage of rifle fire, Ki and Tino opening up from the field to cover Mellon's return.

134

Their bullets flew through the window and riddled the room, further unnerving the four men and sending them sprawling. Even Chadwick was rattled, ducking and hopping while pawing out his gun.

Simultaneously, Jessie was pivoting from Damrow's slumping body, and glimpsing Chadwick bringing his weapon to bear, she quickly triggered again. But Chadwick was dodging the rifle slugs searing close, swinging aside at that moment and catching her bullet in his gunarm. His stubby pistol dropped as he swerved lurching back against Damrow's body, and stumbling, he fell flat on the floor behind the carcass, still yelling to get the bitch.

His four men, harried by the rifles, struggled to obey. But by then Jessie was jumping back into the kitchen, swiveling to face the three gunnies behind her. Alarmed and brandishing weapons, they were coming to help at a slower pace, hesitant to stampede blindly into an explosion they could hear but not yet see.

"Hustle, boys!" Jessie screamed, her shrill adding to the pandemonium. "Mellon's gang is busting in the front door! Hurry!"

They charged past her through the entry. The first took a slug from a panicky comrade in the front room, folding as the second dived sidelong to the floor. The third man balked—but Jessie, using her boot rather than a scarce bullet, kicked him staggering, then hastily slammed and bolted the door.

Chaos reigned in the other room, Chadwick roaring with stymied fury, his men bellowing curses and firing into the door. Crouching low, Jessie seized Veblin's trussed ankles and pulled the marshal across to the corner behind the heavy cookstove, hunkering close to him, sheltered by the iron and out of line with the entry door.

But there were also the rear door and east window to watch, and barely was Jessie settled when some of Chadwick's men appeared at the window. Their blasting guns and swearing howls, the ringing clang of metal as their lead repeatedly hit the stove, made a resonating din. The one noise missing was the one Jessie needed the most, the sound of rifle fire from the wheat; it had ceased as abruptly as it had begun, as though the trio out there had pulled back to safety, unaware Jessie and Veblin were trapped in the house.

A couple of well-placed bullets of her own squelched the gunmen from rising in the window to take aim. The entry door gave, and Jessie put a bullet through a hand groping to pull the bolt. Someone yelped in agony, and the hand was spasmodically withdrawn.

Then the door was smashed in with a chair used as a battering-ram. Now they could fire from the other side of the entryway, but Jessie sent splinters flying, and none was too eager to try for her. They also seemed reluctant to storm the rear door, which was all of two feet from her, and hinged to open back against her corner. The other kitchen window was mostly hidden by the bulk of the stove, and though she couldn't watch it, neither could they get her from it.

Mainly her vulnerability lay in the entryway and east window, and from them both now came a concerted fusillade. Jessie scrunched low to the wall, preferring to wait it out rather than waste her dwindling ammunition, using the time to reload swiftly while their bullets cycloned around her, spraying plaster and wood and ricocheting off iron. Then, their gunfire tapering, came a pause as if the men were thinking, leastwise hoping, that surely she'd been hit.

A shotgun was thrust around the inner edge of the entryway. Jessie angled and shot quickly. Her slug smacked the barrel and spoiled the aim, thunderous buckshot sieving a hole in the wall.

A short lull followed. Jessie took a few moments to cut Veblin's bonds, hearing faintly the mutterings of conversation, the frustrated treading of boots. Chadwick's men were not the sort to die for a cause, much less for a woman, yet they were determined to kill her and the marshal one way or another.

Voices in the front room joined those coming from outside. Then silence. Jessie pressed back, apprehensively watching the openings into the kitchen...Suddenly she sniffed.

"Wood smoke!" she gasped.

It was drafting in the broken east window, swirling and growing thicker as the valley's night breeze fanned a low rosy glow into licking red flame. Jessie, recalling Webster saying they'd been set to torch Lyden's barn, realized with dismay that they'd ignited the house instead, forcing her and Veblin to be burned alive or be smoked out and shot down.

The increasingly smoke-laden air stung her eyes and rawed her throat, making her cough. Sweat ran down her face from the blazing heat blistering the outer walls. She shifted so the stove was between her and the fire, squatting down to avoid the denser smoke and heat higher up, and glimpsed through smarting, watering eyes that Veblin was beginning to stir feebly.

He moaned, wincing as he tried to see. "Jessie?"

"I'm here, Erik."

"Fire...I can feel it, we...can't we get..." Veblin was seized by a choking spasm that shook him painfully. "Get out..."

"Well, we can't stay here," Jessie answered grimly, knowing Chadwick and his men were waiting, guns leveled, for them to flee.

She gathered up Veblin, supporting as best she could the taller, heavier marshal with her left arm straining and her knees almost buckling. It was all she could do to keep her balance, and she leaned to the wall, pushing her shoulder against it to stop from falling over. Dragging Veblin, who was willing but unable to stand upright, Jessie made for the rear door, figuring it didn't much matter if she used it or the front, she'd be greeted with lead.

Wrestling Veblin, she managed to unlatch and pull the door open, the rush of fresher air giving her a respite before death. With the roar of the blaze in her ringing ears, her lungs crying for more air unpoisoned by smoke, Jessie hauled Veblin over the sill—then released him, letting him slump dazed while she hunted for Chadwick's men, intent on taking some with her in her last fight.

Smoke wreathed about her, but nothing like the horror of the kitchen. Her red-swollen eyes cleared a bit, and she thought she could discern vague shapes and flashes ahead. Returning fire, she braced for the ripping slugs that would finish her—but none came, and she paused, squinting disbelievingly. Now, through the lessening vapor, she perceived the shapes were farther than she'd first thought, actually back at the border of the wheat. And above the ominous deep-throated sound of the burning house, she could faintly hear the crackle of gunfire coming from two separate directions, the fringe of wheat and the open barn.

Just one explanation made any sense to her: Mellon was back, and not only had Ki and Tino returned with him, he'd brought some farmhands to help attack the house. They must've been rather shocked to find the house afire, with Chadwick's men grouped outside pointing guns at it. They'd taken full advantage of the weird situation, though, and now were shooting past the house at the barn, where Chadwick and gang had fled for cover and were firing in response.

Hope suddenly swept over Jessie, reviving her lagging strength. She reached for Veblin, turning to shoulder him, then pushed erect and started hauling the dazed, wobbling marshal into the yard.

"There they are, Erik. That's it, try another step, good,"

she encouraged him, then sang out, "Gunther! Ki! Don't shoot!"

Past the bulk of the house with its entire west wall consumed by flame, Jessie heard the whining of Chadwick bullets and saw the ground spitting grit from their impact, but kept heading toward the wheat as fast as she and Veblin could stagger. Mellon's forces evidently recognized them, for intensifying volleys raked the barn, driving the gunnies low, giving her and Veblin time to escape.

It took great effort to hoist Veblin up and over the fence at the edge of the yard. Soon as he landed tumbling, Jessie scrambled between the barbed wire strands, and together they plunged into the concealing wheat. Almost immediately they were met by Ki, Mellon, his foreman and a dozen or so hands, who'd all come converging once the pair no longer needed their protective salvos.

Mellon was grinning. "You got the marshal! Nice work."

Ki also smiled. "We've been worried, Jessie. You hurt?"

"Mostly frazzled," she panted. "Erik's beaten up."

"Erik's fine, thanks," Veblin protested woozily.

A salvo of bullets shrieked low overhead.

"Down!" Mellon yelled. "Where'd *they* come from?"

"The front yard . . ." Tino parted the wheat to stare out. *"Dios!* A whole new mob's ridden in, twenty, maybe more of 'em!"

"Webster," Jessie murmured, then said, "We'd better get going. Lyden's dead, his house is a loss, and we're outnumbered."

With agreement swift and unanimous, Mellon signaled a fighting retreat to their horses, and six men including Tino stayed on the line, just behind the fence, shooting hard to hold the suddenly expanded Chadwick gang from charging the wheat. The rest hurried for the horses, which were a short way back in the field, Jessie mounting behind Ki on his feisty bay, while Veblin was boosted up to ride double with Mellon. Then the other six men ran quickly to them, and the party galloped east for home.

The regrouping gunmen pursued with snarling guns, but the rear guard of farmhands replied with sufficient, if inaccurate, firepower to keep them at a respectful distance. After a mile, the chasing horde slowed and called it quits in a final burst of long-range shooting.

Along the way, Jessie and Ki traded brief accounts.

Ki and Veblin left the slough soon after she had, Jessie learned, and traveled country paths to Mellon's ranch. Veblin, acting increasingly peculiar, rode off at nightfall without explanation, seen only by a sentry reporting in from the west section. Trailing, Ki, Mellon, and Tino found Veblin's horse shot dead behind Lyden's barn, saw the Chadwick gunmen occupying the house . . . and the rest of his story generally confirmed what Jessie had surmised.

"That's what happened," Ki concluded. "But not why it did—why Erik felt so compelled to go to Lyden's without a word to us. Guess we won't know till he tells us. How'd you wind up in there?"

Amused by Ki's puzzled tone, Jessie began by relating her stellar performance as Virginia Arps, her glimpse into Chadwick's murderous character, and her observance of his big surprise in action.

"A field mortar!" Ki blurted, genuinely taken aback. "No wonder they were scared to cross the bridge, and for good reason."

"Unfortunately, Linz is sure he'll have it buttressed by morning," Jessie said and continued telling of the events up to killing Damrow. "I had to; he had a bead on Mellon. I grabbed Erik and got behind the kitchen stove. They torched the house, but you returned in time to hit them and get us out. That's all."

"That's enough, I'd say. More than enough."

140

"Enough for now, anyway," she answered coughing, her talk aggravating her smoke-irritated lungs and throat. "More later."

They lapsed silent, Ki's rugged features set in stern lines, Jessie pressing wearily against his back.

Chapter 12

When they rode into the Mellon ranch yard, employees and children cheered their safe arrival. Mrs. Mellon and Honora awaited them fretfully on the porch, hastening down the steps when they saw the marshal slumping behind Mellon.

"I'm all right," Veblin insisted as he was helped off.

"Sure, you are. You just need a drink."

"He needs a bath, Gunther," Mrs. Mellon stated firmly, a scrub and soak, apparently, her remedies for most human ailments. Deaf to argument, she took Veblin in tow to the bathhouse, to be cured in a nice big tub of clean, steaming water.

The interlude allowed Jessie and Ki a chance to freshen up, Honora informing them that Mama had prepared a wee snack in case anyone felt weak. The bedroom assigned Jessie was sandwiched between Ki's and one given Veblin, the latter fact Jessie learning when a maid entered Veblin's room to fetch clothes for him.

Shortly, they gathered in the dining room. Veblin looked bathtub cured as a broiled ham, had a gauze bandage coiled about his head like a turban, and seemed acutely embarrassed by all of Mrs. Mellon's womanly solicitude and nursing.

The food she set out did not, however, embarrass him. Her snack would've satisfied a cavalry platoon, mounts and all, and Veblin gorged enough for two ordinary people—roast beef, fried chicken, vegetables, jelly and preserves, coffee and pitchers of milk, and warm bread, pie and cake. It was a glory to be ravenous and able to eat; it satisfied the soul, both Veblin's and Mrs. Mellon's.

It also pleased the host, who grinned benifically at Veblin as the last empty plate was removed. "Feel better, Marshal?"

"Yes, sir!" He smiled through swollen lips, his features bruised and cut but appearing contented. "Best meal in ages."

Table-talk had been of this casual sort, a bantering diversion from the looming threat of death and destruction. Small mention was made of the happenings at Lyden's farm, and Jessie refrained from souring the mood with her news of Chadwick's plans—although she couldn't resist telling how Mellon's loan note got torn to shreds.

"Don't that beat all!" Mellon eyed her with amazed admiration. "It was sure sharp of you, Jessie, recognizin' that watermark."

"I didn't."

"Well, then how'd you know how old the paper was?"

"I didn't," she repeated, giving a laugh. "I was bluffing."

This sparked everyone's laughter. Their good humor lasted until after the meal, when Honora and her mother retired, and Mellon and his guests withdrew to the patio. It was then Jessie became somber and informed them of the seriousness of her discoveries.

"By Jupe!" Mellon gasped, stunned. "I rec'lect mortars from the War. The gall, to blow us and our houses up with one! D'you reckon they'd really dare it and be killing women and kids, too?"

Jessie nodded. "Chadwick is determined to finish you all."

"Then we've got to get warning the folks before he hits," Veblin declared. "We'll run 'em out and hide in the fields."

"And get hit there instead," Mellon growled. "The mor-

143

tar'll lob shells at us wherever, keepin' outta our rifle range, leavin' Chadwick's riders nothin' but to come chasin' down our leftovers."

"Yeah, it'll be hard to fight once rolling in action," Ki agreed, pacing near the patio wall. "Chadwick has men and arms a-plenty, and he'll—" Ki paused, as if listening— "he'll guard his mortar extra well now. He might not've tumbled on to Jessie's identity, but he'll know he'd been tricked and'll fear another," Ki continued, moving toward the others. "Still, I may have an idea..."

"Let's hear it," Veblin urged.

Instead of answering, Ki beckoned and glided softly toward an arched opening in the wall. The others, taking his hint, tiptoed after. Then, peering around the archway, they saw Tino a short distance away, crouching against the backside of the wall.

"What're you doin' there, Tino?" Mellon demanded.

The foreman jumped, swiveling. "Why—why—" he stammered. "Why, I was just cleanin' away some weeds for a new flower bed."

"Since when were you demoted to gardener?" Veblin asked suspiciously. "'Specially one not cartin' any tools."

"I'm not doin' the planting, only seein' what's needed."

"What I'm seeing is a guilty conscience," Jessie declared, eyeing the shaken man. "C'mon, Tino, what're you up to?"

"Nothing, I..." Hesitating, he looked down and scuffed his boot. "I can't go on. I... I've been spying on you, Mr. Mellon."

"*You?* I trusted you, and you sold me out?" Mellon roared.

"I did not sell; I did what I thought best for Honeydew." He swallowed, miserable, then rushed on, "It was after Roger disappeared, on one of my rides searching for him, when a coupla Chadwick men waylaid me. One held a gun on me while the other showed me Roger's wallet and did the talking. Said they'd taken him prisoner, and'd kill him if I didn't let them know everything—if you sent for help, for instance, or how us farmers were planning to fight. He said they'd get in touch with me later. They have, same way, coming out of nowhere when nobody else's around."

"Makes sense. As a farmhand, Page'd be out easy to snatch," Ki reasoned. "As Honora's fiancé, he'd be worth holding."

Jessie shrugged, sighing. "At the time, maybe, but Chadwick has the mortar now and is set to strike. Page is of no use to him."

"I thought the same when overhearing you," Tino said glumly. "I fear Roger won't be released alive. It'd be the sore death of Honeydew, if anything such happened. And if I was the cause of it, if I sent men to try to find and rescue him . . . you can see how it was. I was trying to think of a way out, only going along with them till I could. But I can't carry the load alone any longer."

"Well, you're gonna carry your duds alone outta here!" Mellon bellowed. "Spying and conniving! Oughta throttle you! Now, ride!"

"Papa!" Honora cried from the archway. "No!" She hurried up and hugged Tino by the arm, staring pleadingly at her father. "You should thank him, not fire him. He was doing it for me, and for Roger naturally, even at his own sacrifice. Please let him stay!"

"Thank him! It'd be a cold day in Hades afore I'd thank a scoundrelly, ah . . . Hmm." Mellon trailed off in a simmering mutter, apparently reconsidering as some of his anger left him. It was beyond him to refuse his daughter any favor, so grudgingly he nodded assent. "All right. But you're on probation, Tino, y'hear?"

"I hear!" Tino, grinning, glanced at Honora. "I thank you."

145

"Thank my ears for hearing y'all when I went back to the dining room." She squeezed him anxiously. "Where could Roger be?"

Tino shook his head, grin saddening. "If I'd a clue..."

"Does Chadwick's place have an icehouse?" Jessie asked.

"Sure, a good one," Mellon answered. "Leastwise when it was owned by the Odells, who could afford bringing in ice. Why?"

"Well, earlier tonight, Chadwick ordered a henchman to take Erik to his place and lock him on ice with the boy. I know, I know, 'on ice' is an expression and 'boy' might mean anybody, but..."

"But it's a clue," Tino said, heartening. Then he grew sad again. "Ah, but the place is *un rancho del Diablo*, like a fortress. It's guarded heavily and sentries ride the line continually."

"Perhaps not so much tonight," Ki suggested, "not if Chadwick is pulling in men to help protect his mortar, which can win him all the ranches. But even if the devil himself is on duty, it's the most logical place to look for Page, assuming he's still being kept alive."

"You're right, Ki," Mellon said. "I'll round up everyone—"

"No. Just one or two. A few can go where many cannot."

"I'm going," Tino stated. "I've a personal score in this."

The foreman stood taut and his face was like stone, Ki saw, weighing him carefully. What Tino lacked in training he'd make up for in determination, and besides, Ki doubted he'd accept staying behind. "Okay, Tino, as long as you know the way," Ki agreed. "Get a pair of moccasins, a sharp knife, and yourself back here."

As Tino hurried off, Jessie asked Ki, "Were you just gabbing or do you actually have an idea?"

"I hope I have one," Ki said slowly and explained what had occurred to him since viewing the convoy at the slough.

146

He ended by telling Mellon, "If it suits you, we'll work out the details later. But d'you think you can get, oh, two dozen men to join in?"

"More'n that," Mellon replied, chuckling. "What you've in mind is the greatest scrap I heard tell of. Everyone'll chip in."

"No, just select a coupla dozen of the scrappiest sharp-shooters. Tell them to come armed with plenty of ammunition, full canteens, and food. Tell them it could take all tomorrow or maybe longer."

"I'll do it. You give the orders, and we'll follow 'em."

"We don't want to risk any leak, so don't tell them more than that. Except they're to meet here ready to go at midnight."

"Midnight, eh? I'd best get ridin'! 'Bye for now."

Veblin watched him leave, then asked, "What'm I to do?"

"Nothing," Ki replied. "Not yet. Rest, you need it."

"I tell you, I'm perfectly capable of—"

"Now, Erik," Honora soothed, "I'll get you up in time."

"When you do, wake me up, too," Jessie said, stifling a yawn with her hand. "Ki, good luck finding Roger. And your plan sounds fine, considering. It's got to work fast and hard to beat Chadwick, but it's probably the best and only chance to do it. Now, if you'll all excuse me, I don't mind admitting I'm tuckered out."

Stretching, Jessie smiled wearily at the others and headed for her room. Perhaps it was her example which persuaded Veblin, but in any case, as she strolled through the archway she heard him reluctantly say, "Well, I might as well snatch forty winks myself. I'm holding you to your word, Honey-dew, you wake me up if anything happens."

In her room, Jessie opened the windows to let in some air, drew the curtains, and undressed. She would've liked to have gone with Ki, but the demands of human endurance had forced her to pause for rest and to recover from the effects of the fire and the previous night's exhaustive search for Ki. It was this same fatigue which made her decide to hell with it, she was too tired, the night was too warm, and her nap would be too short for her to bother with brushing out her hair and putting on her peignoir.

She slipped naked into bed, feeling the crisp sheets delightful against her bare skin as she relaxed, shutting her eyes. Sleep claimed her quickly, while she was worrying that as she napped Chadwick would be busy with enough men to keep at it in relays.

A tentative knocking on her door awoke her.

"M'God, is it midnight already?" she murmured blearily and shifted around, tucking the sheet to her neck. "Who is it?"

A muffled, "Er . . . Um . . . Ah . . ." came through the door.

"Oh, it's you, Erik. C'mon in, the door's unlocked."

The door eased ajar and Veblin slid inside, quietly closing the door behind him. He was still wearing his gauze turban, but the puffiness of his face had subsided, and he was wearing a striped nightshirt that was far too wide and came only to his knees.

"It's Gunther's. It doesn't fit me," Veblin said, as though reading Jessie's mind. "I . . . I didn't mean to disturb you."

Jessie didn't respond at once, but struggled to sit upright with the sheet draped modestly around her. Veblin was hesitantly padding closer, the short nightshirt twisting about his muscular legs as he moved, emphasizing his crotch area. And watching him with sleep-dimmed eyes, she thought dizzily, *Either Erik's got his gun on under there, or he's hung like a horse!*

Her errant thought caused a slight twinge of self-consciousness to steal through her, and she hastily glanced higher—only to see Veblin's eyes roaming the contours of

148

her thrusting breasts. "Yes. Well, was there something you wanted, Erik?"

"I can't sleep."

"And you don't want me to sleep, either."

"Oh, no, I . . ." He sat down gingerly at the edge of the bed. "No, I wanted to talk, Jessie. I was tossing and turning, and just knew I'd never catch a decent bit of rest until I explained to you."

"Whatever about?"

"Me. Being caught at Lyden's house." He folded his hands and plunked them in his lap, which stretched the nightshirt that much more over the pocket of his groin. Jessie stared, but Veblin, too wrapped up in his confession, failed to see her reaction or the focus of her attention. "I was upset, you going alone to try worming into Chadwick's trust. It didn't seem right. I felt, well, useless."

"But we went over that, Erik. You couldn't do it."

"I know. Only I thought maybe I could do something else to help. I knew that Ki would say the same as you, so I didn't tell him or nobody anything. I just figured the least I'd do would be to spy on Chadwick's setup and how he's got his defenses arranged."

"That's not a bad notion at all, Erik. Why the blues?"

"Because I rode off and, heck, I got turned around. Lost. I wandered onto Lyden's farm accidentally, and 'fore I realized it, my horse'd been shot and I was up to my armpits in gunmen."

He stood then, stiffening his shoulders as though preparing to face a firing squad. Instead he was facing a young woman, whose view of his jutting loins mere inches away was causing her taut breasts to tingle, her rosy nipples to harden involuntarily. From their first meeting in Stockton, she'd been attracted to the easy grace of his motions, the strong muscles flexing in his chest and legs, the hard bas-

149

relief of . . . Whoops! Jessie scrunched her naked buttocks against the mattress in an attempt to quash the budding tendrils of arousal curling in her belly.

"I feel like a lummox, Jessie," Veblin was saying. He paused, his tongue licking his lips as he regarded her . . . and Jessie could sense it now, the desire stirring within him despite his best intentions. He cleared his throat, tried again. "Like a lummox. I botched things up again royally, and I want to ask your forgiveness."

"No forgiveness needed. All's well that ends well."

"Thanks." He continued standing, rooted uncomfortably.

"Was there anything else you wanted to tell me, Erik?"

"No, I guess that's about it."

"Then for heaven's sake come to bed."

He choked. "Don't fun me, like I was thinking to take advan—"

"No?" she cut in, a ghost of a smile creasing her mouth. "It never crossed your mind Erik?" She let the sheet fall free of her breasts. "It's crossing mine, and it's crossing yours."

"Guess it shows, eh." He grinned ruefully, glancing down at his nightshirt perversely tenting out from his loins, and then gazed smoldering at her, his voice husky. "Well, it 'pears I can't deny that if the lady is willing, I wouldn't dislike a kiss 'tween friends."

She gave a long, purring sigh. "The lady is willing . . ."

Veblin joined her on the bed, kneeling alongside and bending to touch lips, kissing her gently, almost teasingly. A breath later he was kissing harder and she was kissing back, and fire was in their mouths. When finally he eased from their soulful kiss, he shifted to suckle each breast, laving the nipple into aching hardness before moving lower to her navel, and then to her love mound, his hands smoothing the sheet away as he wetly progressed.

Jessie moaned blissfully as he parted her legs and slowly

laid his fingers upon her rosy nook. "Pink," she heard him whisper. "So pink and moist and tender delicious . . ."

His mouth pressed hungrily against her crevice, his tongue snaking out to lick its full sensitive length and swirl over the tingling center of her womanhood. Jessie gasped convulsively, but Veblin gave her no respite, burrowing deeper in a prolonged, forceful kiss, whipping his mouth up and down until her hips trembled and her loins throbbed with kindling orgasm. She felt herself on the verge of release, when Veblin raised his head and grinned.

"Now, *that's* kissing," he said, positioning himself between her open thighs. "This boy sure do like tasty kissing." Quickly removing the nightshirt over his head and flinging it aside, he again smiled carnally as he stared at her splayed, glistening crotch.

And Jessie stared at his exposed erection, trepidation mixing with her yearning. "God, it is . . . It's big as a horse's!"

"Naw . . ." He loomed over her, and she moaned, feeling his blunt girth pressing against her anxious hollow, and hearing him add brightly, "But say a colt's, and I'll call it my peacemaker."

"Mmm . . . I suppose that depends on how you spell it," she quipped, her moan becoming a quavering groan as he began to enter slowly inside her. "Lord, I think it should be called a widowmaker."

Chuckling, Veblin lunged.

Jessie sucked in her breath, eyes widening and mouth gaping, shivering from the ecstatic force of his stabbing penetration. She feared she'd cry out and bring the entire household running before he was entirely buried within her. God, he was filling her! And to relieve the strain she spread her legs wider, still quivering as she continued to feel herself stretched by his massive shaft.

He started pumping, tunneling deeply, furiously, hammering her savagely. And she was responding with equal savagery, her breasts trembling to his surging assaults, her internal muscles clinging tautly as he pounded rampagingly far up into her belly. Jessie could feel every tiny fold of her squeezing with each stroke of his spearing manhood, her hips pistoning to match the rhythmic batterings of her flesh, her buttocks grinding lasciviously against the tempestuously rocking mattress.

A tremor began gathering inside Jessie, a warning like the advance of a sundering avalanche. Frantically she raced to meet it, her motions skewering her completely around his plunging shaft. Again she poised breathless, tensing, straining . . .

"Ahhh . . ." She bit her forearm to keep from screaming, her nails raking furrows in the bedsheet. She felt Veblin shuddering, and his seething eruption volcano into her spasming belly. Then gradually they fell limp, Veblin remaining burrowed in her, becoming flaccid, yet still feeling very large to her.

Jessie hugged him when, withdrawing, he pressed close beside her. She stifled a contented yawn, tired as ever and satiated to boot, her sensual fires banked and cool. She closed her eyes.

And dozed.

This time nothing, not even the loss of his warm body when Veblin gently arose to depart, could interrupt her deep sleep.

Chapter 13

The moon was frail, but the stars shed light for traveling, the Big Dipper wheeling in the sky as Ki and Tino pounded across field to hit the road along Chadwick's property.

It had been shortly after midnight when the pair left the Mellon ranch yard. Gathered there had been Jessie, Veblin, Mellon, and his farmers—thirty in number, despite Ki's orders—saddled and eager to commence action.

By then, Ki and Mellon had settled most of the details, just as Ki and Tino had worked out their tactics while waiting Mellon's return from summoning the farmers. Every one of them had joined plan unheard and had arrived with whatever had been requested, such as axes and bucksaws and great coils of rope, Captain Inglenook bringing his cannister of stump-removing black powder.

"Get positioned as quickly as possible, and keep out of sight and your horses quiet. Hold their nostrils if you have to," Ki told them when outlining the strategy. "Tino and I'll catch up soon as we can, which should be in plenty of time."

"How'll we know, if we can't see you?" a farmer asked.

Ki shrugged. "If you don't see us, they won't see us, which's more or less the idea. We'll try to get across afterward, though, and mix in with you. But listen, if we don't make it, do as Gunther here directs. He knows exactly what'll need doing."

"We'll beat 'em, won't we ever!" another farmer exclaimed.

"I hope so. We're sure going to try," Ki replied, mounting to depart. "We've got to stop Chadwick, or he'll poison the whole state."

Now, he and Tino skirted the open roadway, their pace slower so they could scrutinize the wheat-swollen terrain. Ki rode alert, almost as silent as Tino whose manner was cautious and sullen. The foreman did not utter a single word during the entire long ride, not until he drew rein in a scraggly grove near Chadwick's fenceline.

Dismounting, he said curtly, "We hike from here."

"Would you mind spilling what's eating you, Tino?" Ki asked patiently, stepping down to tether his bay.

Tino eyed him sourly, then stooped to remove his spurred boots. "I resent you not confiding in me," he said, tugging on moccasins taken from his pack. "You didn't trust me with your plan beforehand. No, I had to learn of it same time as all the others."

"I'm trusting you on this, aren't I? My neck's in your hands, Tino, but it's just you and me. Look, if there'd be a leak, you'd be blamed automatically if you knew of it in advance."

Tino didn't respond at once, first binding his crisp black hair with a kerchief. "It's true, true as my real anger being at myself. I've been at the frayed end of my tether since Roger was grabbed six weeks ago." He added his hat to his footgear and extended his hand to Ki. "I've been acting *el recto*, the asshole."

They shook warmly. Then, while Tino made sure he wasn't carrying anything that might clink and betray them, Ki muzzled their horses with bandannas to prevent their whinnying.

Keeping low, they crept to the barbed wire that fenced in Chadwick's ranch. Tino took out a pair of wire clippers,

154

but Ki told him no, a hole in the fenceline might be detected. So easing between the strands instead, they ducked into the wheat and burrowed through to gentle rise. There they lay for a moment, picking a route and reconnoitering the shadowed, low-rolling landscape.

Ahead, in an elevated clearing, the ranch proper showed a sprinkling of lamplit windows, but otherwise it was bulked hard black against the softer black of the sky. Surrounding it were dark fields spreading murky and indistinguishable, broken only by the bobbing forms of line riders patrolling the outer fenced perimeter.

When the positions of the line riders permitted, Ki and Tino moved down off the rise to a narrow lane that ran for a while in the right direction. Sprinting hunched and watchful, they made time along the lane until it swerved aflank of an inner fence. They crossed the fence into the next field, then pulled up short.

"What the hell!" Tino swore. "Flowers?"

Indeed, Ki saw, here and for some distance beyond was not a blade of wheat. Instead were tight rows upon rows of thin-stemmed plants, ranging from two to four feet in height, and bearing large, solitary blooms of three to seven inches in diameter. Most were shriveled and faded, the plants following an annual cycle similar to wheat. Yet some were still colorfully white, pink, or purple, and all the more insidious for their innocent beauty.

"Oriental poppies," he replied grimly. "Opium poppies."

"No kidding. Ain't that the stuff you guys smoke?"

Ki had to grin at that, but mirthlessly. "Yeah—and what you inscrutable Westerners sop down in cough syrup and medicinals like laudanum, and refine to inject straight into your veins."

They pressed on toward the ranch buildings. All was silent, save for the normal sounds of nature, the faint sign of a night breeze, the cry of a far-off bird, the rustle of dry fruit pods as the poppies in their path swayed gracefully aside.

Eventually, brushing past the last of the countless rows, they came to a second inner fence. On the other side, they plunged through another, much shorter stretch of wheat. But it served the same purpose as that of the larger first field, Ki realized: as a thick border, a tall hedge to conceal the true cash crop of this farm—and probably of every other farm Chadwick had taken over.

The wheat ended abruptly at a weedy dirt strip which more or less encircled the wide, packed-earth clearing. They stole toward a clump of oleander near the south face of the main house and from that vantage point searched the lay of the yard and buildings.

"I don't like the looks of it," Tino whispered.

Even softened by starshine, Chadwick's ranch didn't appear inviting. What was once the Odell home had the size and style of a small second-class hotel, and now it was where Chadwick undoubtedly entertained many second-rate guests. The long bunkhouses could accommodate upwards of a hundred men, with their own outhouses, cookshack, and messhall conveniently nearby. Numerous other structures were spotted about—barns, sheds, cribs and the like—including a great carriage and horse stable, having an adjacent corral that was presently empty, and an attached building that looked too large to be solely for tack or storage.

Chadwick had done himself proud, hornswoggling the Odells out of this estate, and he obviously aimed to keep what he had and ensure it grew until he'd hogged everything in this region. Guards with carbines or double-barrel shotguns paced around the yard. On the house veranda, a whole squad of men lounged about, armed to the teeth, seemingly relaxed but prepared as the guards to crush any intrusion.

Ki had no way of telling if this was the usual force holding down the fort, or if it had been reinforced, or if, as he'd suggested earlier, some had been switched to help protect the mortar. He was sure, however, those here were doubly alert in response to Jessie's brave foray to the very heart of Chadwick's operation.

"We'll edge around, come in on the stable from the left, where that building is," he said. "I wonder what it's for, if that's where most of the farm supplies are received and shipped."

"Who cares, long's nobody is in it," Tino grumbled.

Carefully they began bellying across the open spaces between points of cover. A parked freight wagon, a rump of shrubbery, even the contour of a slight rise which cast a shadow, took the flattened duo toward their goal. Once they passed the outer line of structures, it was easier in some respects, harder in others. They could make use of the walls to hide, yet the guards were not as readily detected as they'd been against a lighted background.

Darting in among a series of tool shanties, Tino paused at one corner to point out the icehouse—which was beyond the stable and was not a house at all. It fit Tino's previous descripton of being a tiny, slant-roofed shed, like a lean-to, with its front and door facing away and stairs within leading down to a basement cave.

Moving on, they angled to the rear of the stable's attached building, then cut around the side in hopes of locating a way in. This was a side they hadn't been able to see before, but Tino recalled a doorway along it from his prior visits to the Odells. Now they found the side had a recently built loading ramp with padlocked double-doors as well as a regular door added to the wall.

They cat-footed up across the ramp to the door and cautiously tested the knob. It turned, and they opened the door just a crack in order to slip inside. Ki was closing the door, on the verge of relatching it, when suddenly he heard boot-steps and froze.

A guard was nearing the ramp, his approach on the dusty hardpan almost as quiet as theirs had been. He had a wild mop of hair and beard and a heavy build about that of the late, unlamented Damrow and acted unaware but warily awake. He stopped, propped a Damascus-steel cannon of a shotgun against the ramp, and pulled out tobacco and papers. Ki and Tino remained statues not daring to breathe, much less chance the click of a relatching door. The guard rolled a smoke, fired, and puffed on it, then paced on.

When the guard had gone, Ki shut the door and they both sighed relieved. The interior was pitch-dark, as though windowless, so they risked lighting matches and headed along aisles between high stacks of bales toward a connecting door to the stable.

At the door, Ki said, "I'll be with you in a minute."

Tino, grumbling, entered the stable area while Ki struck another match and made a fast inspection of what, apparently, was a warehouse. In one corner he discovered a small office area with a desk littered with various papers, mostly bills of lading for grain shipments scheduled out of Stockton on the Centralia Lines.

What intrigued him more were the bales. Piercing the burlap of the closest bag, he confirmed his worst suspicions. It contained gum opium, the solidified brown residue that exudes from incisions slit in the poppy pods. Assuming, as he did, that the rest of the bales held the same, the amount of gum opium stuffed in this warehouse was staggering, enough to give half of North America a long period of dreamy hallucinations.

Ki was on his fifth match when he joined Tino in the stables. Tino had chanced upon a candle stub, and by its feeble glimmer was backing horses out of their stalls. While he finished releasing them, Ki chose the three seemingly strongest of the over two dozen roaming free. Then scrounging up gear, Ki saddled the three and slip-knotted their reins to posts near the closed stable entrance.

This was, as Tino had put it, their insurance policy.

They snuck out through a side door up by the front, hearing the muffled thud of hooves as horses wandered the aisles inside. The noise didn't sound much different from horses moving restlessly in their stalls, and it should pass muster unless a guard peeked in. Or so Ki and Tino hoped, as they hugged the dirt toward their next objective, a corn-crib. From there they dashed down an alley separating the rear of a hay barn and a fenced practice corral.

It took them quite awhile of such fits and starts to reach the sloping backside of the icehouse. They could no longer hear the horses, only the soft footfalls of prowling guards and the murmuring voices of the men on the porch. Crouching low, they inched toward the front and were pushing flat against the corner when they heard an unmistakable clink of glass against metal.

Again breathless, motionless, they listened acutely.

Nothing. Ki peered for an instant around the corner and drew back, holding up two fingers, then making the gesture of a man chugalugging out of a bottle.

"Celebrating our funeral, huh," Tino mouthed in reply. He eased out his revolver, partially thumbing back its hammer.

Ki shook his head and dipped his hand into his vest, easing forward for another glimpse, counting on this being the side away from lamplight and the moon to keep him concealed.

One gunman was sitting on a stool, leaning with his back against the icehouse door. He had a pint of whiskey in his hand and was offering it to the second gunman standing next to him. The second guard put out his hand to take it, then hesitated uneasily as if sensing something were wrong.

Ki became part of the earth, willing himself invisible.

The first gunman wiped the mouth of the bottle and thrust

159

it out again, and this time, shrugging, the second gunman accepted it. He raised it to his lips for a hefty swig, while the first man went to stroking his chin. The first was stroking and nodding approvingly, when there came a feathery whisper from the corner, and a needle-tipped dagger suddenly pinned his hand to his throat.

The drinking man choked, dropping the bottle. "Wha—" he began, as his buddy rolled off the stool. He abruptly shuddered, gurgling, puzzled about the knife blade which had slashed clear through his throat; he actually had time to finger the bloodied dagger before crumbling alongside the first man, both now mutually dead.

And by that time Ki was there, Tino crowding his heels and muttering, "We're handy with blades south o' the border, but you—"

"Stop babbling and help me move them inside," Ki hissed intently, retrieving his knives. "Don't forget the stool."

Bodies were shoved aside to get at the door, Ki lifting the latch and wincing as it creaked rustily. The hinges squealed even louder when he yanked open the door, but the horrendous stench that roared out almost blew them away.

"This isn't an icehouse," Ki managed while gagging, forcing himself to haul in one of the bodies. "This's an outhouse!"

Tino wrinkled his nose as he followed with the other man and the stool. "I'm scared to light my candle. The air might explode."

Light it he did, after the bodies were dumped and the door reluctantly closed. They were on a short landing with stairs going down into some ominous black pit. Descending, they found the reek growing palpably stronger, becoming nearly thick enough to slice. Then they reached a square, underground vault. It was lined with stone blocks, the floor shaped to drain the melting ice into a cistern. The cistern had an iron grate, and around two bars of the grate was padlocked a chain, the chain trailing off somewhere into the noxious gloom.

A voice quavered, "Is it food? If not, go away!"

"*Dios!* Roger? Roger, this's Tino. Come here."

The chain rattled and slithered as a man stumbled toward the candle, blinking the way a nocturnal animal would when facing harsh sunlight. His gaunt face was pale, a sheen of sweat covering it along with a six-week growth of whiskers. His eyes had receded into their sockets, but brightened considerably when they saw the foreman and Ki. His clothing was filthy and tattered, especially his right pantleg, where a leg iron was fastened around his ankle; but they didn't drape baggy as if he was emaciated, his youth and good health having allowed him to hold up through his imprisonment.

"I ain't going to ask how the hell you got here," Page said. "Just get this chain off me. Some guard or other has the key."

Ki loped up the stairs to rifle pockets, hearing Page's echoing voice ramble on under the emotional stress of his rescue.

"The lobos caught me out in the fields. But I got away from 'em right at first, Tino, almost. I kicked the hoss of the weasel riding beside and watchin' me. The hoss started buckin', and I lit out lickety-split. Till a lasso sang out and pulled me outta my hull like a cow in a boghole. Next thing I knowed I was here. Been here ever since."

"Won't be much longer, Roger," Tino said cheerfully.

Ki returned, Page shuffling to meet him by the steps. "Don't wantcha goin' back in there more'n you hafta," Page said, as Ki hunkered to unlock the leg iron. "That's where I've been havin' to . . . Well, anyway, there's a pile of it su-preme."

Ki quietly introduced himself, and then they ascended to

the landing, Page weak but steady on his legs. When asked, he explained he'd nothing else to do except walk around, so he'd been walking for the last six weeks.

"Good, because we're sneaking out on a long hike across the fields," Ki told Page. "If we're spotted, though, we'll never hold off this gang afoot. So be ready to break for the big horse stable."

Edging the door ajar and checking the area, Ki motioned for Tino and Page to follow him. They glided toward the kitchen end of the nearby main house, treading swiftly yet quietly, while keeping eyes and ears peeled for any hint of their discovery.

They never saw or heard him coming.

They couldn't. Totally without warning, the bearded guard barged out the pantry screen door, toting his double-barrel shotgun in one hand and wadding a jelly sandwich in his mouth with the other. He was startled as they were by plunging smack-dab in front of them, but despite that, despite his size, he was fast.

Tino stabbed to draw, but the guard was quicker. Before Tino touched palm to revolver, the guard had his weapon up and braced with both hands, finger squeezing the first of its triggers.

The guard was quicker, all right, but Ki was quickest. He moved with a tigerish lunge, a snap-wristed *shuriken* flashing straight through the air and slicing in under the guard's right arm, sawing deep into layered fat. It threw the guard off balance. He bellowed with the shotgun, which tore a gaping hole in the ground and severed the feet of his boots and some of his toes with buckshot.

Tino now fired. The guard reeled on his bloody stumps and dropped to his knees, howling, a dazed fog seeping over his eyes. Tino fired again, not at the guard, but hitting another gunman who'd come racing to see what was the matter. He went down, yet behind that man were others, with more in back of them, alarmed by the thunderous gunfire.

"The stable!" Ki shouted, wheeling that way.

Men were trampling from the veranda, appearing at doorways, lunging from between buildings, converging out across the entire yard.

Hesitating an instant, Page snatched up a shotgun, cocking the second trigger while turning to run. Tino yelled, "Watch out, Roger!" and shot a third time. A gunman gave a screech of pain and lurched aside, clutching at his punctured shoulder. And Page, falling in with Tino and Ki, let fly a riveting blast that gutted another man and seriously wounded a companion trotting alongside.

Dark, raging confusion erupted in the yard, as ducking and zigzagging, they sped for the stable. Lead searched after them, but their pursuers were too madly dashing to aim effectively, the bullets flying off-target, some close, some wild. Headlong they dived through the side door, bolting it instantly, knowing they had scant time before the descending gunmen would surround and storm from every angle. And by that time they'd have to be gone, or be dead.

"Somebody unblock those main front doors!" Ki ordered, sprinting past the three saddled horses. "I'll be with you in—"

"I know, I know, in a minute we don't have," Tino moaned.

It took less than a minute, Ki having memorized locations of supplies before. Swiftly he collected an old horsehair saddle blanket, a lengthy piece of rope, and a kerosene lantern that sloshed full. Around him, the freed horses were snorting restive, prancing skittishly as savage barrages tore into the walls, some of the heavier-charged bullets drilling through.

163

He streaked back to the saddled horses, where Tino and Page were already mounted with reins in hand. On his way he'd tightly knotted one end of the rope around a corner of the blanket and now emptied the lantern's reservoir of kerosene over the blanket. With reins and rope in hand, he climbed asaddle the horse they'd been anxiously saving for him and gave them a grin.

"All set?"

"Hours ago! *Mio Dios!*"

"Set aside so you won't get caught in the rush," Ki replied, swinging his mount about and heading down-stable again. When he'd shouldered through the increasingly spooked horses and got to the rear, he struck a match and tossed it on the blanket. The kerosene-soaked horsehair caught with a high-flaming burst. His horse took one look and went berserk.

And so did every other horse in that stable.

"Hiiiyaaa!" Ki shouted, heeling his mount into a dead heat gallop. It bucked and winged to get rid of the fire on its tail, which panicked the horses in front all that much more. "Hiiyaaa!"

The horses stampeded crazily, whinnying and pawing and crashing out through the unblocked front doors in hysterical frenzy. They collided pell-mell with a host of gunmen, who were just launching an assault on the stable. Pistols roared, men scrambled, and the horses ran amuck. Behind all the hullabaloo rode Tino and Page, then Ki on his frantic mount, still scrambling in four-legged flings to escape the flapping, crackling terror that insistently chased it.

They veered across the yard toward the fields, Tino in the lead now, knowing best how to go. Page followed close, eating dust but sticking like glue, both men hunching low to avoid being hit by some of the cooler-headed gunmen

164

firing at them. Ki paced a near third, and to hell with staying down, his concern was staying in the saddle and heading his mount in the right direction. And following fourth was a lengthening trail of fire.

Farther in back and going nowhere were the horses milling and romping insanely in among the buildings, plus the gunmen, who were busily dodging the horses, not knowing where to turn but figuring movement would keep them from being trampled better than standing still. As the trio escaped into the wheat, there was a violent scream from one of them who'd figured wrong.

The blanket, with its blaze whipped and fanned to a livid fury, kindled the parched chaff. Ki, glancing over his shoulder, saw their backtrail was burning and spreading like a smoldering wake. And yonder in the clearing, ribbons of smoke were squirreling upwards from the eaves of the stable, the hay and dry timber inside it having ignited on his way out.

When they came to the first inner fence, Tino leaped from the saddle and swiftly cut a gap in the barb wire with his clippers. Then they forged bounding through the rows of dry poppies, which caught fire as readily as the wheat. Nearing the next fence, Ki let go of the rope, reckoning the blanket had done its job. His idea had been to cause a diversionary stampede; burning the fields and torching the stable and warehouse were grateful extras, but unplanned— nothing this spectacular could've been. Three for the price of one, at the cost of a permanently paranoid horse. Not bad.

Before long he was wondering if it was all that good, either. The stable and warehouse were geysering flames and mushrooming clouds of smoke—including smoke from incinerating gum opium. There wasn't enough wind to push the clouds anywhere, so likely the gunmen underneath were comatose by now. But if a breeze picked up and flowed this way, Ki soberly questioned whether any of them would navigate out alive. Or wish to.

Burning fields didn't need wind to spread, however, just more tinder. That there was plenty of, and already a broad mass of landscape lay scorched, the fire advancing faster than a man could run for safety.

"Move! Move!" Ki called urgently.

They shoved on with flagging horses to the outer perimeter, not worrying about the line riders, who would surely have been drawn to the fires. By the time they approached the grove where Ki and Tino had tethered their own horses, their shirts were singed and they had to keep beating sparks out of their hair. Behind, the stable and warehouse roofs were collapsing in a shower of flame, and the fields were raging so fiercely, the very air seemed to be burning.

Hastily Ki and Tino stripped the Chadwick steeds and slapped them galloping free. Then tightening cinches and removing bandannas, they mounted their horses and, with Page, headed for the road.

"Well, this part of the set-to is practically wound up," Tino remarked when they arrived. "I think the road's enough of a break to stop the fire from leaping across onto Mr. Mellon's property. It ain't a tree-crown fire or nothing like that."

"Roger," Ki said, "you look a mess. But I suppose you don't want to wait to get cleaned up before seeing Honora?"

"Hell, no!" Page declared eagerly. "How is Honeydew?"

Tino squirmed in his saddle, but pasted on a smile and answered heartily, "Why, missing you sorely, Roger. As you may've guessed they would, some folks rumored you'd spied on Mr. Mellon and turned bad because the raiders hit us the night you vanished. But Honeydew stuck by you. She thinks the world of you, Roger."

166

"Gee . . ." Page sighed. "C'mon, then, let's get going."

Ki shook his head. "We can't. We've still got a few chores, so you go on ahead and we'll be back shortly. Oh— and Roger?"

"Yes, Ki?"

"A word of advice. Stay downwind of her as much as you can."

Chapter 14

Ki and Tino left the road to cut their own path northwest. They had a fair distance to travel and were reluctant to tire their mounts by making haste—which they couldn't have done anyway, their trail twisting and turning as they tried keeping to cover, ever alert against unpleasant surprises.

Eventually they reached the southern back rim of the slough and paralleled it riverward along the bank. All the way the bridge was visible, an inky slash across the flat basin of the slough. By halfway they saw the fireglow of the convoy's encampment and the lampglow emanating from Estero. For quite a way the town itself was hidden, having been built back from the slough to discourage chronic sinking. Finally, though, they approached where Ki could distinctly make out the dominating thrust of the Roundheeler and the Indianhead warehouse.

"We've ridden far enough," he said. "We'll walk from here."

They secured their horses in concealing brush, climbed down the bank, and set off again toward the bridge. They felt relatively safe from casual observation, but continually searched for guards of patrolling sentries. Nary a sign of one could be glimpsed.

At one point, Tino ventured, "Chadwick's not taking much precaution. Either his mortar isn't there, or he doesn't care."

"It's there, and he cares it might be in danger," Ki replied.

"But he's too smug to care how that danger might strike. He arrogantly believes holding *his* mortar with *his* gun-toadies makes *his* power ace-high. Well, may his conceit be his downfall."

The nearer the bridge they got, the worse it got. They were forced to churn through viscid gumbo that slorped with each step and weasel through tall nettling grasses and slimy plants, occasionally snagging on sunken limbs or hidden roots and always thrashing at greedy insects that whined tormentingly.

At last they ducked in among the bridge pilings. After a short hunt, Ki located where Captain Inglenook had stashed his cannister of black powder. With it had been left a couple of blasting caps, a combination fuse cutter and crimper, and a huge coil of double-tape fuse, fashioned from numerous smaller lengths, each neatly crimped in a line so burning would be even. All the accessories were tucked in a black leather satchel, a school kid's kind, with a strap for slinging it over a shoulder.

Captain Inglenook had come through; now it was up to him.

Ki slung the satchel over his shoulder. "I'm leaving now, Tino," he said, clutching the cannister under one arm. "Remember, dig in and stay put. And don't try finding any of the others."

"No socializing, I'll remember." Smiling, Tino watched Ki begin scaling the pilings. *"Buena suerte!"*

Climbing to the supports under the bridge superstructure, Ki crouched in their vee and inspected the timbers. As Jessie had earlier informed him, workers had jammed short logs under the horizontal beams to add stability. They were there in place, but they wouldn't be doing much stabilizing. The fifteen or so farmers concealed around this end of the bridge had seen to that; they'd sawed most-way through them and the uprights and had pretty well weakened anything else they could lay blades to.

Ki grinned his thin, metallic grin, easing out around the supports so he could continue on. Then, abruptly, his grin faded.

From his position, he had a straight view across to the north bank under the bridge. It was a bit too far and dark to see clearly, but it was easy to make out the blaze of lanterns and torches down over there, indicating something was going on. His plan hadn't included tampering with those supports—too many gunmen, too many risks of even chance discovery. Yet had it been tried, and now discovered?

It made his task all the more important.

Clasping a better heft around the cannister, Ki started a one-handed swinging from crossbeam to crossbeam, crawling over slick wooden braces, fingers groping, ankles locking, as he strained to keep from falling. It was slow and perilous going, the muscles of his arms and legs soon tiring, but eventually he drew up into the crotch of the beams supporting the main uprights.

Below, where the upright poles rested against the flat outcrop of rock, he could see where the workers had lashed logs to the two uprights. The logs were longer than those used under the support beams, but were still too short to reach to the top. And the workers had been unable or unwilling to hazard a climb to this roost. The beams up here by Ki had been left alone.

Not for long. Gently, so as not to topple, Ki shifted the satchel around front. He took out a blasting cap, crimped it to one end of the fuse, then pried open the lid of the cannister, stuck the cap inside, and gingerly reclamped the lid, not wishing to sever the fuse. He dallied a little slack in the fuse, and straining to reach, wedged the cannister under the beam closest to the middle of the bridge. Softly he withdrew his hand; the cannister remained, stuck tight.

He played out more fuse as if preparing to go. But he didn't go; he couldn't, not while whatever was happening over on the far bank was in his way. He squinted to pierce the gloom, focusing on the light and hoping to see the men around it.

He managed to perceive a tall man in a military cap, evidently the head honcho, Linz, of whom Jessie had spoken. Linz was squatting down, conversing with what looked to be workers.

Ki waited, watching. Linz began nodding and didn't appear to be in a big stew. Okay, so maybe they don't suspect anything, maybe they're doing a final examination, a checking of details. But would Linz demand another, more thorough examination at the very last minute? Ki had been counting on human nature. They'd reinforced the span, and from what Ki could tell so far, the farmers had been careful not to leave warnings of sabotage.

Ki waited longer. His breathing seemed pounding in his ears, and a strut creaked ominously when he shifted his squeezed position under the beam. Linz was up now, still talking.

Ki waited still more, gazing about distractedly. The shadows cast by the growth along the slough were dense, intractable. The bridge itself was reflected on the slough water below, not by moonlight or starlight so much as by a horizontinging vortex of orange and white, the distant inferno of Chadwick's farm.

Finally, centuries later, Linz and his cohorts went up the bank with their lanterns and torches and disappeared toward the convoy's encampment. He waited yet again, to be damn good and sure everybody had gone and wasn't coming back. Then, unreeling the fuse as he went, Ki worked his exhausting way to the bank, staring downward every so often at the gelatinous surface of the slough. Coming to the north bank, he shinnied down the supports and stood poised under the bridge for a moment, listening.

He could hear the raucous voices from the convoy, but nothing close by, nor were there any signs of life along the bank. He moved to his right, diligently covering his unwinding fuse by squishing it into the earth as he stepped over to where a tree had slid down and settled, roots upended. He went behind the spill, the ground slick and spongy, his rope-soled slippers making soft sucking noises as he knelt and cut the fuse. He left the end exposed where he could easily find it, wormed the satchel in among the choking ball of roots, and climbed the bank.

It took him close to half an hour to scout cautiously the area and locate Jessie. He knew he was disobeying his own orders by finding her, but he supposed that was his prerogative. Anyway, they'd previously agreed in private where she'd be hiding, and besides, he was hungry and she had all the food.

She was not far from the bank and, he thought, too close to the convoy on the road. The depression she was snuggled in, borrowed carbine at her side, was an irregular square bordered by ferns and other low-growing plants. Some sun-withered scrub and a spindly thatch of saplings served as her screen from the mortar-carrying wagon in front of her. The wagon, in turn, was screened by too many gunmen sitting around drinking too much beer, which could result in any one of them, at any time, blundering through her sapling fence for a place to piss. Ki made a note to refresh Jessie's lessons on choosing hiding places when this was over.

He slithered close to her through the grass and ferns, seeing her turn warily and almost get to her knees. Her pistol clicked to half-cock. "Shhh," he whispered, sliding in by her.

Jessie squirmed to face him, her grin like a knife wound as she realized she might have shot Ki unintentionally. "I was wondering if you'd show up," she said, her tone low. "What happened? What's that big fire? Do you know anything about it?"

"They wouldn't feed me, so I torched the kitchen."

"Oh, that's it. You came to beg." Jessie produced her canteen and an oilpaper packet, out of which came a cold meal of salted meat and bread. "Now, Ki, sing for your supper."

Ki sang as he dined, relating the harrowing events at Chadwick's ranch and the rescue of Page from a very rank dungeon.

"I only hope we have as much luck on this caper," Jessie said when Ki had finished. "I thought thirty of us would give Chadwick a real run for his money, but I'm not so sure any longer after seeing all the men he's collected. Why, it looks like a convention for killers out there, Ki."

"If it goes off—*when* it goes off, Jessie, the odds will more than be evened. We'll have 'em in a crossfire, in shock, floundering around in muck up to their armpits. Where's Chadwick?"

"I don't know. He's been in and out all night. I think he's been told it's his place that's burning down. Last time I saw him, about half hour ago, he looked fit to be tied. Where're you going?"

"I just want to keep an eye on my things," Ki replied, turning to snake back through the grass. "I'll be back soon."

Ki returned to the bank to make sure everything was secure and hadn't been disturbed or discovered and to study the approach to the trail to the bridge. He saw Jessie again after that, but kept returning to the bank at frequent intervals through the rest of the night, while the gunmen were dozing and even Jessie was slumbering, girding for the big morning ahead.

As red tinged the eastern sky, the gunman began stirring up and about, and Ki could smell meat frying over cookfires.

173

From the bank he now could see Estero, its fringe of shanties nearest the slough, the roof of the Roundheeler and one end of the warehouse. In due course he also could see twelve or so riders crossing over from the town, appearing dispirited and deadbeat, more like stragglers than fighters . . . or perchance more like men who'd been futilely struggling to contain a runaway fire.

The only one sporting any sort of gumption was Chadwick, who sat ramrod stiff in a black cutaway suit and derby hat. He looked decked out enough to join a fancy celebration, but his face looked too ferocious for any celebration too jolly.

After the gang went by and mixed in with the convoy, not much occurred until the sun had lost its initial red tinge. Then the impromptu encampment began to fold; fires were doused and horses were saddled, and the mule teams were harnessed to the wagon.

"Here they come," Ki murmured under his breath, and keeping very low and stealthy, he crept down the bank to the fallen tree. Retrieving the fuse, he took it with him to the bridge, once again climbing the supports to crawl in under the already packed beams. There he stayed, tensed, while the convoy gathered ready.

It was a massive escort those two wagons received, riders ahead of them, riders flanking alongside, and a long, disjointed tail of riders bringing up the rear as they moved out toward the bridge they had reinforced. The advance guard moved slowly in accord with the wagons, the hoofs of their mounts ringing as they started across. Next came the groaning creak of laden wheels, as the great wagons hauling the mortar and shells approached the bridge.

Ki sat unmoving, listening to the first team of mules set foot on the north end of the main span, and the wheels protested mightily on the upgrade while they bumped along behind.

174

Waiting as breathless and hidden as Ki, fifteen farmers on each bank eased hammers and levers of their weapons, as coldly determined to stop this horde as Chadwick was to stop them.

Near Ki's perched vantage was a side railing made of wooden lengths. It was flimsy and only about three feet high, and Ki could see through it the bent heads of the second team of mules, pulling the mortar wagon closer to the center of the span.

Linz was up there, wearing his cap and tunic, leading the mule team confidently onto his checked and tested re-engineered bridge. Farther back, beside the wagon bed itself, rode Chadwick and Sheriff Dexter. Their voices and tone were recognizable to Ki, but their words were lost in the thudding of hundreds of hooves resonating hollowly under the bridge.

It didn't matter what they were saying, Ki thought as he slid down the support; there was no mistaking the cruel, fierce ugliness about Fenton Chadwick. Hunkering with the fuse, Ki took out his waterproof box of matches and discovered it wasn't completely waterproof. Sulpher matches were hell to light when slightly damp, but after a few failures he got one to flame. As he coaxed the fuse to burn, his lips formed Chadwick's name, but no sound came out. Those gunslingers up there didn't know anything about what was waiting for them.

The punk end of the fuse streaked up the supports, burning faster than Ki had estimated. He turned and lunged from under the bridge, risking being spotted by some rider—who couldn't do anything about it right then, anyway—as he raced for the tree and dived behind it. Eddying from the bridge were sounds of jingling chains, the clack of horse shoes. Someone coughed. A horse snorted. Ki smiled slightly, coldly, eager now that this was truly the beginning of the end.

175

And concealed by the bank, Jessie glimpsed Ki's head-long sprint and knew there was no turning back . . . that the only chance to end Chadwick's menace cold in its tracks was irreversibly on target. As impatient as she felt, she forced herself to remain still, only shifting to better sight her carbine, her senses honed to as keen an edge as one of Ki's knives. *Now . . . Now . . .*

As if on cue, the black powder cannister detonated with a brilliant, deafening shock wave. The midspan of the bridge was peeled hurtling up and out in suddenly sprouting in-candescence, the plankboards, beams, horses, and riders cycloning about in belching thick clouds of smoke. Into the hole the charge had punched, adjacent pieces of span col-lapsed, widening the crumbling gap, embers glowing like a terminal disease.

"The mortar," Jessie moaned. "The mortar!"

The wagon to which the mortar was fastened appeared unscathed at first, not having been quite yet to the center of the bridge. But swiftly, inexorably the hole grew as more debris broke loose, swallowing the wagon's front team of mules, and the mortar's great weight did the rest. Screaming, the harnessed mules plunged down toward the water. The mammoth wagon slid to the edge of the tipping plankboards, two wheels went over, and as the entire bridge sagged, groaning with ear-splitting noises, the mortar broke loose from its bindings and chocks and rolled off into the slough.

Linz, the wagon driver, and what looked to be Chadwick and Sheriff Dexter went with them. Jessie couldn't make out too clearly what was happening to whom out there, for the bodies of man and animal cascaded into the water in confusion and were hidden by murky powdersmoke. And a second later, the whole bridge fell.

The heaving, suddenly unpropped midspan put a twisting strain all along its length, and at the south end, the posts which had nearly been cut in two splintered completely apart. Those in front of the wagons had been pressed into startled bunches to gawk at the wreck of the field mortar. As the bridge tipped nearly to form a right angle and splashed heavily in the bed of the slough, they were catapulted, some pinned under the collapsing structure. Screams and curses rose as they went down. Horses were kicking and lashing out dangerously. And there was little help at hand, the small number of gunmen still on the north side being blocked by the lack of a bridge.

Before the Chadwick forces could recoup from their shock, Mellon fired into the air, signaling the second part of Ki's plan. Out from along both ends of the bridge came the farmers, those on the north side driving the gunmen on the bank before them into the slough or into hell, it didn't matter which, with lead-spitting revolvers and carbines. As that bank was swept clean, those on the south bank opened rapid, deadly fire. The gunmen were caught between crossfire, and though they tried to whirl and flee, they found themselves mired in the slough's muddy bed. They fell where they struggled, to sprawl in the shallow water.

Jessie, in a one-knee shootist's crouch on the north bank, heard a big buffalo gun bellow from the other side and saw a gunman reel in his stuck boots and hinge over. Linz was shouting orders out there, his stentorian tones caustically loud even above the din of gunfire. Sheriff Dexter was tripping splat-flat with almost every other step, his face lathered by muck yet visibly stricken with stunned fear. She caught a glimpse of Chadwick flailing about, his black suit dripping brown and his derby long gone. She shouldered her carbine for a solid shot at him, but a bullet out of nowhere skimmed past her ear, making her wince reflexively and miss. Chadwick swerved behind some debris before she could reaim, so she glanced around to see who'd aimed at her and realized then that the gunmen were attempting to rally.

They had the manpower and weapons to launch a withering counterattack, and they did in spite of being stranded in the slough. Barricading themselves behind dead horses and portions of the bridge, they began unleashing a torrent of lead at the banks, sending the outnumbered farmers back or down low.

But the farmers responded with resurgent determination, knowing this was truly a do or die situation for them. From the banks they sent crashing volleys, catching the gunmen from one side, one angle or another. Riderless horses plowed screaming in all directions, adding to the melee of exploding guns and agonized howls, both sides mixing it almost point-blank, making the slough run red from the horrible slaughter.

Jessie saw the sheriff wade through it untouched, his constant slipping saving him from being drilled a dozen times. He was gradually heading toward the north bank, not quite by her, but down farther where Marshal Veblin had stationed himself. She glanced toward him and was puzzled momentarily to see he had ceased firing. He was merely kneeling there, carbine in hand, listening as she was to the terrible screams of men shrieking. And seeing, as she was, gunmen trying to break free, becoming hopelessly bogged, piling up against one another in a smashing tide, with the blaze of gunfire mushrooming down into them from the banks.

A kind of horror hit her, and now she understood.

Sheriff Dexter reached the water's edge and crawled up the bank, swearing hotly. Veblin reached, and his steel fingers gripped the lanky sheriff's arm, dragging him over the crest.

"Marshal, I—I—"

"Dexter, I arrest you in the name of the State of California." Veblin rammed his revolver against the sheriff's nose. "Tell your men to surrender: They're surrounded, and it's death if they fight!"

Dexter was more than convinced as he felt the cold steel of the muzzle against his shrinking flesh. "Aw'ri! Aw'ri! Throw down, boys!" he squawled, when the firing permitted it. "The marshals have got us! They're here! Hundreds o' them!"

Many heard him and they threw down their weapons. Only those off to the sides with a chance to make it sought escape by scrambling, crawling, half swimming to some distant bank. Most were caught in the crush, but some succeeded—

Such as Fenton Chadwick and Linz.

Ki had been keeping his eyes sharp for one or the other of them and had caught flashing glimpses of each man separately out in the slough. Now for the first time he saw them together, wading and stumbling through the morass, groping for the bank farther up by the river. Ki realized that Chadwick and Linz, knowing they didn't have a chance, were trying to get out of the hell they'd each helped to create—and that their bolt for freedom might just succeed, if they could reach the slough's mouth and duck upriver.

He launched into a run, hampered by the turgid mud.

Spotting Ki, Chadwick raged obscenely. His arm that Jessie had wounded was now bandaged and taped inflexible in his coat sleeve, but his left hand swung pointing a good-sized revolver. Linz too was gripping a pistol, and turning to see what Chadwick was cursing at, he immediately opened fire. Chadwick was an instant behind him.

But Ki came charging on, the notion of allowing them to escape making his flesh feel cold and grainy. Then Chadwick hit the bank, slid, and fell to his knees. Linz nearly bumped into him, but sidestepped and scrambled up the bank. They were almost within range of Ki's weapons, and Ki struggled to close those few paces. Chadwick, straight-

179

ening, fired and slipped again from the recoil, but forced Ki to dive, the man's offhand shooting accurate enough to send a bullet grazing his hair.

Linz, clawing to the top, scuttled away from the bank on all fours and disappeared. Chadwick, sensing he'd never get up there before Ki got to him, dipped into a watery thatch of cattails behind an earthen mound. And Ki, flat on his belly in the muck, knew he was an exposed target, as Chadwick stuck his gun out of the cattails and triggered from behind the mound. The hard, deadly roar of heavy calibre timbre bounced eching off the bank. Mud sprayed Ki's face, and he swiped at his eyes with his shirt sleeve, figuring what the hell, no use lying here and dying.

He rose to one knee, and a slug plucked at his pant leg. Then he was vaulting forward again, hunching low, his fingers darting into a vest pocket. Chadwick leaned and inched a bit higher to get in another, better aimed shot, but Ki kept on sprinting as his hand snapped a *shuriken* into the cattails. Chadwick groaned, and Ki could hear the flopping and threshing in the water as though someone had hooked a big fish in shallows.

Ki plunged to his belly again at the edge of the mound and crawled cautiously forward to the cattail thicket. Scattered gunfire still burst from around the bridge, but it all seemed faraway and in some other world to Ki. In his world there was only himself, and Chadwick, and a small pool of brackish water between them. He eased nearer, gripping his short, curved knife.

Chadwick was on his side, his chin turned and dragging in the plant-shadowed water, and one hand held a Colt .44 straight out and leveled at Ki's face. Ki stabbed out, slashing while he rolled wildly to one side, the .44 blasting in his ears. Chadwick squirmed and coughed, then rolled over and triggered a bullet drilling into the water near Ki's left ear. Still grunting and muttering curses, Chadwick tried to lift his revolver up to a level with Ki's head, his hand faltering, the gun tilting.

Ki dragged himself within a foot of Chadwick's face. The eyes were sunken and invisible, and under the mouth the water was darker, the darkest color of all. Chadwick coughed and sagged a little, trying to keep his chin up high, his mouth and nose from sinking down too far into the drink. And all the while he was concentrating on his pistol, trying to raise it that necessary bit.

A hard man to kill, Ki thought, but he's getting there. It was about over, which didn't give Ki great pleasure, only relief.

Chadwick's mouth opened, and red froth bubbled. "You're a fuckin' li'l squint-eyed turd, and I'll de-ball you yet."

Ki reached out and pushed Chadwick's face under the water. Chadwick didn't have enough strength to struggle at all.

"So," a voice above him said, "it's now for me to do."

Craning, Ki looked up at the crest of the bank. "Linz."

The military cap clung tight and wet to the convoy leader's damp hair. The double-breasted tunic was ripped, missing buttons, and splattered with mud. But when he turned his face up to the dawning sun to laugh, the saber scar seemed to glow with victory.

Linz aimed his pistol stiff-armed and precise. Dimly, like something faraway in a dream, Ki could hear the gunfire tapering to a few erratic shots and screams of surviving men and horses and could smell the aftermath of cordite drifting over the slough.

"You're through, Linz, finished." Ki grinned up. "You and your plot with Chadwick are as sunk as your damn mortar."

"Stalled, perhaps. Enough to want this satisfaction."

The pistol was steady, trigger squeezing back for a point-blank shot. There was no place for Ki to hide, no time for him to counter. Then, in that last instant, another voice sounded sharp and clear from behind the vengeful man.

"Go to hell, *Herr* Linz!"

A flame-lancing roar thundered out over the bank. Linz made a lot of noise when he hit the pool of cattails, but after that he didn't make any noise at all. Jessie appeared at the bank edge, carbine leveled in case a second bullet was needed, looking calm, resolutely calm.

She has a knack for seeming calm, Ki thought, and still grinning, he said, "Okay, now can you help me up out of here?"

With a laugh, Jessie placed her carbine down and gave Ki a hand as he climbed the bank. They started back toward the bridge. A riderless horse galloped past them, red foam drooling from its mouth, its eyes crazed and rolling.

When they arrived, they saw that the farmers were disarming the surrendering gunmen. There was no more fighting, no more resistance. The living remainder of the horde was crushed, all idea of attack driven from their stunned minds. After a moment, Jessie and Ki located Mellon conversing with Captain Inglenook, who'd apparently had some artillery experience during his service and had forded the slough to take a gander at the fallen mortar.

"And you're sure that danged cannon is busted a-plenty?" Mellon was asking as they approached. "That no leftover nightriders can drag it ashore 'fore we know it and put it to use?"

"Swear on the Bible," Captain Inglenook replied. "The gun carriage is smashed, and the whole business is full of water and goop. I think the sightin' mechanism is broken, too."

Mellon nodded, then smiled at Jessie and Ki. "I can never thank you two enough. And that goes for the rest of us, by Jove."

"No need to thank us, Gunther. After all, we were acting

in our own interest," Jessie replied lightly. "I believe you shouldn't have any more trouble shipping by Indianhead." She gazed about, her eyes warm with approval. "We're glad to have come. You've got a nice area here with lots of nice folks living in it."

"Salt of the earth," Captain Inglenook said proudly.

"Let's hope other folks appreciate it, too," Ki added, "and that you all live in peace."

Jessie murmured agreement to that, but already her mind was thinking ahead. There was yet another fight to be waged, and for all the peace now here, the dangerous life beckoned.

Chapter 15

It was a grim moment when, the next morning, Jessie and Ki stared through the entry gate at the Willabelle mansion.

As soon as practical, they had left the gunfray at the bridge and returned to the Mellon ranch for their belongings, a lunch far surpassing Mrs. Mellon's previous meals, and a seemingly endless round of congratulations and farewells from visiting farmers. What with one delay and another, they wound up riding to Sacramento through the dead of the night.

Now, arriving at the Willabelle estate, they viewed the grounds beyond basking in yellow sunlight, the air sweet with the perfume of flowers and shrubs. It looked tranquil and innocent, but Jessie wasn't fooled. Nor was Ki, who also felt reticent.

"Jessie, maybe we shouldn't be so hasty barging in," he said. "All we can do is accuse her. We've nothing on her."

"Nothing? I've a half-page entry in my notebook on Linz alone. He was in the cartel up to his saber scar, and that's plenty of evidence she's a member, too." Jessie turned, scowling. "She set up my ambush at her own dinner party, sent fliers offering a reward to kill us, bankrolled Chadwick's attempt to turn the San Joaquin Valley into a giant poppy farm, supplied him with a mortar and gunmen, and that's just for starters. The Widow Willabelle is the mastermind behind this whole infernal affair!"

"All circumstantial. We don't have a scrap of proof tying

184

her directly to any of it. Why, even that gum opium is legal."

"It shouldn't be. But even so, it was being shipped out falsely as grain on her personal freighters. That was the key, you finding those bills of lading for her private Centralia Lines."

"What I'd like to find out is where to and why. There must've been more opium stored than this country uses in a year."

"My hunch is she was transporting it to be refined someplace. As part of a cartel operation to spread the stuff wholesale, add it to tobacco, spike food and drink with it—whatever possible to turn us into a nation of addicts, sapping our strength, our character, our moral fiber to resist the cartel's conspiracies."

"No proof of that, either."

"Then let's go get some," Jessie replied tersely and swung open the gates. Striding swiftly, they went up the drive to the front door, keeping watch for servants such as Hubert and his Austrian pistol. But the residence remained stone quiet, almost as if slumbering, its windows curtained and unlit.

Jessie knocked, but received no answer, so she tested the handle and found the door locked. "Around to the rear," she said.

Leaving the porch, they circled the house and discovered the dining room doors were also bolted. Without ceremony, Jessie took a pace back and kicked her heel through one of its small panes of glass. Then, gingerly reaching through, she snapped the lock and stepped inside.

The house was like a tomb.

Ki shrugged. "Well, we could wait till someone returns."

"Let's get cracking while we wait."

Quickly they set to searching the rooms. In a very short time two facts became apparent: The house was empty, and so was every drawer, closet, desk, or cubbyhole where incriminating evidence might be found. Nowhere were there any clothes either.

"We're in for an awfully long wait," Ki said disgustedly. "No one's going to return for a long while, if ever. They've gone."

Blind rage engulfed Jessie. Mrs. Willabelle had been forewarned, probably by telegram, and had prudently pulled out for fear Jessie and Ki wouldn't be deterred from lack of legal proof. And Jessie, knowing the cartel as well as she did, anticipated a fruitless hunt for the widow, Mrs. Willabelle having managed to disappear from the face of the earth by now.

In an attempt to mollify Jessie, Ki said, "That ol' bat will turn up eventually, and we'll nab her then. Meantime, look what we've accomplished. Chadwick and Linz are dead, and the cartel plot's been skunked. Mellon and his farmer friends are alive to reap their wheat and to make some profit for Indianhead along with themselves. Honeydew will undoubtedly run off with an itinerant carpetbag salesman, saving one of those two young swains a mistaken life. They're all living, Jessie, and taking hold again."

Yes, Jessie thought as she calmed, as long as people like Mellon and his type would live, the good fight would be fought and won. And it had to be fought, constantly, for there was always unfinished business when it came to the cartel.

Watch for

LONE STAR AND THE APACHE WARRIOR

thirty-seventh novel in the exciting
LONE STAR
series from Jove

coming in September!